Private Wolf

Black Hills Wolves 54

By
TL Reeve

This book is a work of fiction. Names, characters, places, and incidents are the products of the author's imagination or used fictitiously. Any resemblance to actual events, locales or persons, living or dead, is entirely coincidental.

Copyright © 2016 by TL Reeve
ISBN: 978-1-68361-061-8
Cover art by Fiona Jayde

Published by
Decadent Publishing Company, LLC

Look for us online at:
www.decadentpublishing.com

~A Note from the Author~

Dear Reader,

The Matchmaker subseries...wow. When I was first told that Miss Fern and Miss Claire would be two of the matrons, I was blown away. Kole's story (*Omega's Heart*) sent me down the wonderful road of meeting these two women. They were spunky, full of mischief and I couldn't get enough of them. They were already setting people up, asking questions and doing what good matrons would.

Now, they're working in a team, and oh wow. I am so proud of *Private Wolf*. So proud to be a part of the Matchmaker subseries of Black Hills Wolves. I hope you enjoy Brie and Shawn's story. I will make this promise now, yes, Tinks, Ginger, Sarah and Jason will all get their stories told, I am working on them slowly but surely.

A little hint: Sarah's will surprise you and Tinks...well...there's a certain biker with her name tattooed all over him.

And, who is this Orion Davis? You'll find out soon enough. *wink, wink*

Until next time, happy reading!

TL

Dedication

To my family and friends, thank you. To my Black Hills Wolves family, thank you for the opportunity to bring Shawn and Brie to life along with the opportunity to work with the matchmaker ladies. This is freaking awesome!

Prologue

"Where is Claire? I thought she'd be joining us today?" The bell over the door of Los Lobos Books and More jingled as Lonnie, Miss Fern, and Miss Kathy stepped into the shop.

The snow had finally let up, and the sun warmed the frozen ground, giving way to yellow dandelions and sprigs of dark-green grass. Water from the rapid thawing dripped from the eaves, splashing on the wildflower seedlings. Miss Fern smiled. Another winter survived and new beginnings blooming everywhere.

She loved the spring. She loved the scent of everything coming to life—rejuvenating after a long, frozen slumber. Earlier, Fern had enjoyed watching a herd of deer frolicking behind her house while small fawns took their first tentative steps out into the sunlight. Of course, Chris, her son, came bounding out of the woods toward her house in wolf form, scaring the poor little deer away. The lug. He was so much like his father, it amazed her—especially when he was hungry, and she'd have breakfast waiting.

"This is a secret meeting. I wanted to talk to all of you without Claire being privy to our conversation" Fern made her way to the front counter to place the banana bread and lemon bars near the register.

She glanced around the store and a welling of pride filled her. Since the twins bought the shop housing the bookstore, they'd come a long way. The hardwood floors were completely redone in a deep-walnut lacquer. Three quarters of the shelving units were in place and, last week, Kole had installed a tiny wood stove, along with a couple of comfy oversized chairs and a throw rug, creating a reading nook for adults. It also gave the pack somewhere to go to forget about the tragedy over the winter.

Too much death. Too much loss. Nevertheless, it brought the pack closer together, which they needed now more than ever.

"Why? What has she done now?" Kathy took her seat at the table in the back room. They had an hour before the twins would arrive and start asking questions about their little get-togethers.

"Did she get into trouble with Joe?" Lonnie grabbed a bottle of water out of the small fridge Kole kept stocked for them. Then she held out a second in offering. "Did he spank her?"

Kathy laughed. "Wouldn't be the first time."

Fern chuckled, taking the proffered water. "Not in the least. Then again, Joe hasn't let her out of his sights ever since the happenings of late."

"He always tended to be a little too protective of her," Lonnie said.

"Not like all of our mates aren't the same way. I swear Henry wanted to keep me chained to a chair," Fern quipped.

"You let him, too, didn't you?" Kathy smirked with a knowing glint in her eyes.

"I prefer not to kiss and tell." Fern lifted her chin. Seconds later she began to laugh then waved off the direction their conversation was heading.

Their sense of community was what the pack had been missing for so long. Friendship. Laughter. Love. She soaked up the comradery between the women before tapping her finger against the table, calling their meeting to order. Finally, after the murders, the Hills were returning to their version of "normal." Members steadily returned home, and those who'd stayed close to their lands were coming out of hiding.

As mated females, they understood the value of having partners in their lives along with a nurturing, loving pack. So, the desire to share their life experiences drew them together for one goal— revitalizing the pack. Their conversations about helping the pack find its footing and bringing out the goodness within them led to a brilliant idea.

Some of the wolves found it difficult to break out of their shells, while others returned to a town they'd gladly left to escape the terrorism of living under Magnum's reign. Breaking the ice, so to speak, became a slow, painstaking endeavor. Most maneuvered around each other, never really settling down. Others seemed to take to finding mates like ducks to water. When Fern pointed it out, the ladies agreed something needed to be done to give those wayward wolves a shove in the right direction.

So, every week, they gave each other updates

about who might need help and who was finally adjusting. This week, Fern wanted to help her nephew, Shawn Blu, and Claire.

Shawn had returned only a few months prior, a little worn around the edges and cynical to boot. Surprising Fern by showing up on Christmas day, he stood on her porch, arms wide, a megawatt smile on his face, but she'd seen right through it. His light-green eyes held knowledge older than him, along with a wariness she'd noted several times with returning members.

"As I was saying, Claire needs our help, and I believe I have the perfect solution. We'll call it two birds with one stone." Fern cracked the seal on her bottle of water then took a sip. "My nephew came home on Christmas day, and he told Henry and me what he did in the human world for a job. I think we can utilize his skills and find his mate at the same time."

"I'm all ears." Lonnie sat back in her chair and kicked her legs out, taking up a relaxed position. "How do you plan on doing this, and what does Claire have to do with your nephew?"

"Shawn is a private investigator. In Chicago, he had an office. He used his skills as a tracker to help humans find missing loved ones, among other things. Claire's niece has been missing for several years, as well as her son and daughter. I think my nephew can help Claire find Brienne." She took another sip of her water then placed the cap on it. "I heard from a little birdie where Brienne might have gone."

"By little birdie, do you mean Tinks?" Kathy arched her brow.

"The girl has trouble written all over her," Lonnie

4

snickered. "She's always been one to put her neck on the line for the females. Fearless is her middle name."

"Yes, she is," Fern agreed. "Tinks gave me a general idea where she could be, but I want him to speak with her. She might open up to him a little more."

"Really?" Lonnie leaned forward. "Claire has missed Brienne something awful since she disappeared."

Fern gave a solemn nod. "I know."

"So where did Tinks say she got off to?" Kathy asked.

"Minnesota."

"What?" Surprise lit Lonnie's words. "How did she get so far away?"

"She could have been killed." A small growl rumbled from Kathy.

"Now, now. We all get the circumstances of why people left and why they stayed away. Terror is an ugly beast; we've all experienced it at one time or another in the last ten years. Brienne did what she thought was right at the time."

"True," Lonnie acquiesced.

Kathy grumbled, "Do we have anything else besides a hunch?"

"No." Fern grinned. "I want to send Shawn after her."

"Do you think he's her mate?"

"I believe so," Fern said. "Before the pack went downhill, Brienne chased after Shawn like a lovesick puppy."

"Infatuation can mimic mating in certain instances." Kathy shrugged.

"Yes," she replied. "But, they are...were different.

I think, if what I saw all those years ago is right, she'll willingly come home and rejoin her pack."

"And if not?" Lonnie questioned.

"Maybe, he can at least bring Brienne home to see her aunt and uncle. I think Claire would love to have a small portion of her family back in her arms." In fact, Fern *knew* her best friend would be over the moon at having her niece home.

"Then I believe we have a match—"

The bells over the front door jingled, and the scent of a familiar wolf filled the room. Ginger gave them a curious look. The little omega seemed a bit lost since her brother mated almost a year before. Her reluctance to show her true self had grown worse since the murders and bothered Fern. After seeing how her brother bloomed with the love of his mates, she'd have thought Ginger would desire the same. Instead, the girl hid even more.

"Should I even ask why you're here earlier than normal?" Ginger's amber eyes filled with cautious curiosity.

"Reading club, girl," Fern held up her book. "You should join us sometime. Orion Davis is an amazing writer."

"Yes, he is," Miss Lonnie agreed. "Did you know humans write about us? How curious, I say."

"Oh yes." Fern nodded. "His descriptions are close to the truth. Makes you wonder if he comprehends something he shouldn't."

Ginger snorted. "I'm sure he's got a vivid imagination, Miss Fern." She glanced away. "I see you've brought more treats for our customers."

"Banana bread and lemon bars."

"Well, I guess we'll settle up with you at the end

of the day." Ginger nodded at the women before making a hasty retreat.

"She needs a good kick in the rear to get her out of her head," Kathy said.

"Another project for another day." Fern smoothed out a crease in the tablecloth. "Shall we get to the business at hand?" The ladies nodded.

"I say he shows up wherever she is and drags her home." Lonnie made a yanking motion with her hand. "Surprise the shit out of her."

"I believe there are a few mates around here who'd do the same." Fern laughed.

"Your Henry, for starters," Lonnie teased.

"It is one of the many things I love about him." A wistful sigh passed Fern's lips.

"I know what you're thinking about," Kathy added with a wink.

Fern shook her head. "Look at us, carrying on like a bunch of new mates."

"Clucking hens, is more like it," Ginger called out, as she passed them, headed for the storage area.

"Hush, child. Your envy is showing," Fern admonished.

"Sorry, I thought I tucked it in today," Ginger popped off. "My bad."

"One day, child," she chuckled softly. "One day."

"Perhaps, but until then...." Ginger shrugged. "How come you don't have your books open?"

"What?"

"You said you were talking about your book." Ginger pointed to the paperback by Fern's hand. "But, you don't have it open."

"Oh, we're gossiping, first." Fern waved off her question. "Then we'll discuss whether Emma-Lou got free from the evil Conroy's clutches. I still say you should join us."

"Mm-hmm. I've seen what happens when you gossip." Keep me out of it. I don't want any part of your shenanigans."

"Yes, child," Fern grinned over the lip of her bottled water. She watched the little omega walk out. "Put her on the list."

"Done," Lonnie said.

"Good," Fern inclined her head. "So we're all agreed. Shawn is going to bring Brienne home."

"Agreed," they chorused.

Chapter One

Shawn Blu walked into Los Lobos Café and spotted his aunt at a table near the far wall. In front of her sat a paperback book and a mug, along with a pastry. Behind the counter, Ero took the order from a new female. Her long dark hair was pulled into a messy bun, and her gray eyes glittered with—arousal? If the other wolf noticed, he appeared indifferent to it. *Oh well.* Bypassing his normal routine, of ordering coffee and Danish, he marched over and sat at the table where his aunt waited. Fern glanced up at him. Her warm, affectionate smile greeted him.

"Good morning, Auntie." He leaned in and kissed her cheek. "That twinkle in your eye says you're up to no good."

Fern laughed and patted his hand. "I have a job for you."

A job. Why hadn't she mentioned it last night when he came over for dinner? Why did they have to meet in the café? "Okay. What is it?"

"Well, technically, it is two jobs...."

"Okay."

Ero approached with a cup in one hand and a sweet treat in the other. "You didn't order. I see why now." He grinned then winked at Fern.

"I didn't want to interrupt your time with Cynthia," Shawn teased. "She's interested in you."

"Don't I know it." Ero frowned. "But there's...the spark's not there." He glanced at his brother, Luc, who sat in his usual spot.

"Say no more, I understand." He did, too. They were waiting for their perfect mate. Might be a while, but Shawn had a feeling it would happen. "Thanks for the coffee."

"You're welcome."

Taking a sip of the piping hot brew, he waited for Ero to leave before returning to the conversation with his aunt. The way Fern watched him—assessing him—left him uneasy. "Should I be afraid of what you're going to ask of me?"

"Never," she assured him. "In fact, you'll win tons of brownie points with Miss Claire if you do this for me."

Shawn took another sip of coffee then nodded. "All right. But, if I do happen to get into trouble, which I am really sure will happen, I'll tell Henry."

"Deal." Fern pulled a small picture out of her purse and slid it over to him. "Ring any bells?"

The scent of lilacs and morning dew enveloped him before he even acknowledged the person staring at him. Curly flame-red hair and bright, sparkling blue eyes gave way to full bow lips and dimpled cheeks. *Brienne.* She couldn't have been more than twelve or thirteen in the picture. "Brie," he whispered. "Did something happen to her?" He hadn't seen her around town, but it didn't mean anything. She could have a mate and be staying on the outskirts.

"No, nothing happened to her." Fern took a sip of her tea. "A year after you left, she ran away."

Stunned, Shawn let out a breath. *Ran away?* The atrocities in the pack were widely understood. The way Magnum tried to destroy everything good about their home and their people. It'd been one of the reasons he left. But, Brie wouldn't leave without saying good-bye or telling people where she was going.

She had a heart of gold and a loyal streak a mile long. *Maybe she left because of her loyalty.* She couldn't support an insane alpha, any more than he or the others. "Do you have any clue where she went?"

"In the beginning, no. I'm still not sure. Tinks gave me a state, but nothing else."

Shawn nodded. "A state is a good start. I have contacts. Which state is it? If I'm successful in finding her, what would you like me to do?"

"Bring her home to Claire. My best friend, though she may not say it or show it, misses her family. Misses her son and daughter. If I can help her in some small way, I will."

A tear rolled down his aunt's cheek, and he wiped it away. "I'll find her. I'll go talk to Tinks about it."

After his parents disappeared, Fern had taken Shawn in. In those first few months, he searched everywhere for them, but he never found them. If he sat long enough and thought about it, he'd guess it was what prompted him to be a detective. Strange, how things happened sometimes. With his skills as a tracker, it was a no-brainer when he left home. Didn't mean setting up his business happened instantly, it took years. The human world rules and laws were more extensive than his pack. He'd needed to go to school. Get a license.

By the time he started practicing, he'd gained a reputation for being fair and for finding a missing person or someone who skipped out. He helped anyone, even if they couldn't pay.

"What did you say to my mate to get her all teary-eyed?" Henry stepped up beside her.

"Nothing. I think she's going soft in her old age." He winked at his aunt.

"Hush." She swatted his hand. "Tinks has the information for you. I told her you'll be coming to see her soon."

"Tinks?" Henry narrowed his eyes. "What do you want with her?"

"I'm helping Fern out," Shawn assured him.

"Oh." Henry relaxed and took a seat at the table. "Is it one of her schemes?"

"Schemes?" He cocked a brow at his uncle.

"She's always up to something lately. I can feel it in my bones."

"You feel everything in your bones," Fern muttered.

"Watch it, mate."

"And on that note, it's time for me to leave. I'll go talk to Tinks, and hopefully by tonight I'll have some news for you. However, like I tell everyone I work with, don't get your hopes up."

Fern smiled and gave him a small nod. "I understand. Tinks is living with her sister out on the pack border."

Shawn inclined his head. "Thanks."

***

The rambling shack sat three miles from the road leading to the state highway. Smoke billowed from the chimney. Chickens wandered around the yard, pecking at the ground, while a woman collected eggs from a small henhouse a few feet away.

Bobbi. Tinks's aunt stuck her head out of the chicken house. Her eyes squinted in the mid-morning sun. Her black curly hair was piled on top of her head in a messy bun.

Shawn pulled his truck into the driveway and stopped a little way from where the fowl roamed in the front yard. Bobbi lifted her hand in greeting as she stepped down the ramp of the coop. "Well, I'll be damned. I heard rumblings of your being home." She walked over to him as he got out then wrapped him in a tight hug. "What brings you out here?"

"I was hoping to talk to Tinks. Is she around?" He followed her toward the house. Silver dappled her long raven hair, and she walked with a slight limp. *What happened?*

"Yep, she's inside. We were just about to sit down to lunch. Would you like to join us?"

"Sure, I'd be glad to." As they entered the house, a little boy with dark hair, blue eyes, and dimples hopped up from the porch and darted inside ahead of them.

What he'd thought was a fire going in the fireplace was actually an open-pit grill they'd created in the kitchen. Clay and rock expanded outward about ten to twelve inches from the hearth then formed a small oven/cooktop facing the window. The extra room gave the ability to make a flat cooking area while still allowing the smoke to travel up the flue out of the chimney. The succulent scent of sizzling deer meat filled the air. Tinks, lost in her own little world, danced around as she flipped the steaks. The boy grabbed her arm. "Mom, we have company."

Tinks stilled. "We never have company."

"Not even old friends?" Shawn stepped forward. "How rude."

She turned slowly. Her honey-colored gaze filled with shock. "Well, aren't you a sight for sore eyes."

"Pfft. You've known I was home for a couple of months now. Don't act so surprised."

"Guilty," she laughed. "What are you doing here?" She handed Bobbi the tongs then tucked the boy into her side. "Jordan, this is my friend, Shawn Blu. He's Miss Fern's nephew."

The boy looked familiar, but Shawn couldn't place him.

"It's nice to meet you, Shawn."

"Good to meet you, too, Jordan." He grinned.

"He's my son." Nervousness tinged Tink's words. "If you're wondering."

"I believe 'Mom, we have company,' gave it away. You're mated?"

"It's complicated," she hedged. "Sit and you can tell me what you need."

"Why do you think I'm here for a favor?" He cocked a brow.

"No one comes out here without a reason," she answered. "Plus, I talked to Fern last night. I had a feeling you might be here today."

"She wanted me to help her find Claire's niece."

He shrugged. "I could never tell her no."

"She'd never let you say no," Tinks corrected him.

"That, too. She's under the impression you might have a starting place for tracking Brienne down." Out of the corner of his eye, he saw Bobbi pull the tin foil-covered potatoes from the embers of the fire. "My aunt wants her best friend to be happy."

"Brie left for a reason." Tinks tone was matter-of-fact.

"I'm more than positive she did," Shawn replied.

"What if she doesn't want to come home yet?"

"It's her choice. However, I'd like to talk to her anyway." He accepted the plate Bobbi handed him. "Thanks."

"Come on, kid. This isn't a conversation for you." Bobbi ruffled Jordan's hair.

Tinks kissed the top of her son's head then waited for him to exit before resuming their conversation. "She's not close by, heck, she might even be farther away now. She didn't keep in contact with me. Can't really blame her."

"Still worried about Magnum?"

"I think so." She frowned. "No one has been able to tell her the news."

"Fear does crazy shit to people." He cut into his steak. "If she's still worried about what could happen to her if she comes home, she'll never open the door and take a chance."

"Don't I know it," she muttered, before she began to eat. "I often wonder if I'd tried to keep up with her, or I'd had an inkling of an idea of where she was going once she made it to her first destination, things would be different."

"Perhaps. But, it might have put you on Magnum's radar, and it looks like you have a very big reason to keep your secrets."

"When she left, she told me she was going to Minnesota." Tinks took a bite of potato.

"Minnesota?" Not what he expected to hear. Lucky for him, he'd worked a few cases there. "She didn't happen to mention a city or town, did she?"

"No."

Shit. "Okay, I've found people with less information."

"You're pretty confident." Tinks pointed out

"I've been doing this a long time." It was part of what made him an excellent tracker. If Brienne wanted to hide, she'd choose the smallest town and try not to raise anyone's suspicions.

"Well, if you can get her to return, I'd love to see her." Tinks gave him a smile.

"I'll be sure to make it happen. Thank you for lunch." He got up, then took his plate to the sink.. "Later, you'll tell me about Jordan?"

"Maybe."

***

Minnesota, of all the places to go. At least in a big city like Chicago, he had reliable service. Here, at his Los Lobos kitchen table, or anywhere in town, if he breathed wrong, he lost the signal. Watching the bars on his phone dance, he prayed for at least two bars. He could deal with a weak signal.

He turned to the left a hair, and the bars settled into position. Two. He scrolled through the contact list and pulled up Lance Wingham's phone number.

Shawn had dealt with the alpha of the Rosewood pack on a missing child case he'd worked on. A little girl from the next town over had been taken from her home in the middle of the night. The suspect's vehicle was found on the side of the road, a mile from pack lands. The doors were left open, and a few feet from the truck, the responding officer found a small stuffed animal.

Lance met Shawn at the border. After a short negotiation, the alpha allowed him to search the area, with one stipulation—he went with him. They worked together tirelessly and then, as the sun went down, the fates smiled upon them. The little girl lay huddled against a stump, shivering, the suspect nowhere in sight. Twenty-four hours, later Shawn handed the little girl off to her relieved and grateful parents.

After two rings, the alpha answered. "Lance."

"It's Shawn Blu. Do you have a minute?"

"Hey man. It's been a while," the alpha said. "Sure, what can I do for you?"

"I'm looking for someone. She's been gone for about ten years, and the last anyone in my pack heard, she was in Minnesota."

"Minnesota is a big state. Do you happen to know where specifically?"

"No." Shawn rubbed the back of his neck. "No one is sure of where she went. At the time, it was a good idea, not so much now."

"Shit, man." Lance snorted. "Nothing like finding a needle in a haystack."

"I have something. It's not much, but it might help."

"Hit me."

"She's got fiery-red curly hair," Shawn said. "Her

name is Brienne Talbert."

"Hmm," the alpha murmured. "Let me get back to you after I check around with a few people."

"Great," Shawn answered, checking the bars on his phone again. "I've got shitty coverage where I am at the moment. If you can't get ahold of me, I'll get back to you."

"Thanks."

The next morning, he woke to the buzz of his phone. Voicemail. Shawn scooted up in bed before grabbing his phone. He slid his finger across the screen and hit the message icon. Lance's voice filled the line.

"You're in luck. One of my trackers believes she's here in town. Has been for a while. If so, she works at Lucy's Diner and, if you hurry your ass up, you'll be able to see her there tonight."

Shawn couldn't believe it. Brienne may have been there when he worked the missing girl case. He couldn't believe he hadn't seen or scented her. He listened to the message several times before saving it and getting ready to leave. He should have told his aunt he had a lead, but he had to be 100 percent sure he was going in the right direction. If he didn't find Brienne, he didn't want to disappoint Fern. After packing his bag, he took a quick shower then headed out. Next stop, Rosewood, Minnesota.

Chapter Two

"See you next week." Brienne packed her bag and stood after her professor dismissed the class. Her shift at the diner started in a couple of hours, so she needed to hurry—which meant eating on the run once again. However, after work, she didn't have to go anywhere for a week. She planned on taking the first week of her summer break off to relax. She hadn't done anything of the sort since leaving home. With only a couple of months of school left, she could unwind a bit.

Walking out of class, she headed to her car. The breezy Minnesota spring weather had slowly given way to warmer, summer-like temps. Of course, after dealing with -30 degrees off and on for eight weeks, she welcomed the heat.

When she'd left Los Lobos, she'd had to make a decision. Go east or west, but don't stay too close to pack lands. Otherwise, Magnum's mongrels would find her. She'd been scared—alone in a foreign world. She'd been afraid of what would happen to her if

Magnum ever found her. In such a state, she'd hopped the first Greyhound bus leaving Rapid City within fifteen minutes, never checking out her destination.

Once she was settled in Rosewood, she thought of sending a letter home to tell her aunt she was okay. The idea of Magnum intercepting the missive prevented her from following through. Though, if the alpha showed up there, Lance would have dealt with him. He'd given her the protection she needed after she approached him and explained why she fled. He'd also helped her get a job at his sister's diner while never pressuring her to join his pack.

Lucy was a blessing. She helped Brienne get into school and worked her hours around her classes and study time while she worked toward her master's degree. They'd become fast friends, even when others thought her a threat, especially the females. More importantly, Sasha. For whatever reason, the girl got it into her head Brienne was trying to take Lance from her.

She snorted.

Brienne had a mate and planned to look for him once she finished school.

She promised herself she'd make it through college then contact someone within the pack, probably Gee, and see if they'd heard from Shawn. Last year, she'd come close to going against her rules and calling the old werebear to hear a familiar voice.

It'd been after a particularly bad day. She'd worked a double at the diner and, of course, Sasha showed up to throw her weight around. The girl sat in her section then proceeded to make her life a living hell. After Brie tried to deal with her for an hour,

Lucy stepped in and allowed Brie take the rest of the night off while she dealt with Sasha.

After that night, it only got worse.

Brienne didn't understand the girl's hatred. She'd never experienced anything like it. The women in Los Lobos huddled together, trying to protect one another. The viciousness...the spite. She couldn't handle it. Even now, Sasha gave her a hard time. *Can't satisfy everyone, Brie. Might as well get used to it.*

She pulled into the parking lot of the diner and found a spot near the back door. After grabbing her apron, she closed her door and walked inside. Plates clattered together as one of the men pushed a tray of dirty dishes into the dishwasher while Claudia stacked the clean ones on the counter to be used to deliver meals to the appropriate tables.

Fifties, Rock-a-Billy music blared from the stereo system Lucy put in last year to replace the old, rundown jukebox. Friday nights were always busy. Throw in the fact it was a nice day by their standards, and the place was slammed.

"I'm here, Lucy." She stored her stuff then wrapped her apron around her waist.

"Great." Lucy grabbed two plates off the line. "Help Ashley. She's got your section and her own. We're short-staffed. Also, you have someone requesting your presence."

"Who?" Brienne followed her out. Her mind raced. No one from school knew where she worked. Could Magnum have found her? Her stomach dropped. *No. You know better. Who would tell him where you are?* Maybe a Rosewood pack member? *But why?* None of this made sense.

"I'm not sure," she replied. "I've been too busy to get chatty with him. He's at table five, and he's already been waiting about twenty minutes for you."

"I'll deal with him first." She split off from her boss.

As she approached, the scent of sandalwood and cedar filled her nose. Her steps faltered. She knew the scent. Missed it. Broad shoulders, curly blond hair, and thickly corded muscular arms were all she could see, until he turned his head. Shawn. His strong jaw framed his straight nose and full lips. Yearning filled her, and her wolf reveled in the fact her mate sat nearby. He shouldn't be here. If someone had followed him and word got back to Magnum, she'd die and so would Shawn because he found her. Paranoid as it sounded. Her fear of the vicious alpha she escaped, ran deep.

"Shawn," she whispered, afraid if she uttered his name any louder, he'd disappear or worse yet, not be him.

The corner of his lips kicked upward as he turned in his seat. "Aren't you a sight, little Brie?"

Her heart gave a heavy thump. "Why are you here?"

"I needed to talk to you."

She licked her lips. Fear gripped her insides. Her gaze bounded off of the exits while also scanning the area for any threats. "Listen to me. Get into your car and leave. Don't return, either. It's not safe here for you or me."

Shawn shook his head. "No one is going to hurt you."

"Don't do this to me. It'll kill me if Magnum comes after you." Her hands trembled as anxiety rushed through her.

"Listen to my words," he murmured, taking her hand in his. Warmth pushed away the nervous edge. "Magnum is dead."

The chattering of the diner grew distant. Magnum was dead? How? Who? She shook her head. *No, it's a ploy.* Something new the vicious alpha started, a new way to torture everyone. She shook her head. It couldn't be real. A dream, for sure. A demented, sick dream she'd wake from any minute now. Brienne closed her eyes and counted to ten. When she opened them, she'd be in bed, waking up.

Brienne cracked her eyes open. The diner returned in roaring clarity, and Shawn still sat in the booth next to her. "No. You're lying," she snapped. "He's not dead. Who'd kill him? Who'd save us?"

"Drew," Shawn answered. "Can you sit with me?"

"No. I have to work, and you need to leave."

"I'm not going anywhere," he growled. "I'm staying here until you talk to me."

Rubbing her forehead, she sighed. "Fine, it's your funeral. At least I have protection here. A lot more than you do."

"It's going to be fine. When you're done with your shift, come talk to me. There's so much you need to hear." The way he pinned her with his light-green gaze—the absolute conviction and sympathy in his voice made her want to believe him.

Could she trust him? He was her mate, after all. Still, what if he'd been given some cock-and-bull line as well? What if it was all a ploy to get the females back to the pack? Which would mean he'd be working for Magnum, too. Her thoughts weren't rational by any means, but someone like Shawn didn't just show up.

Her head spun, and her stomach turned to water. "I'm not sure if I should."

"If you don't like what I have to say, I'll leave, and you'll never have to see me again." He leaned back in the booth, giving her space. "No one will find you either. I promise."

She scented no deceit. "One conversation." She kept her distance. "Then you leave and never return."

"One conversation." He nodded. "It's good to see you again, Brie. I've missed you."

She'd missed him, too. "Order something so you can stay."

"Whatever the special is," he said. "Haven't you missed me?"

Yes. "It's good seeing you, too. I'll get your order."

Brienne walked away from his table. She wanted to climb up into his lap and rub all over him. She missed him. She'd wondered where he went and what he'd done with his life since leaving the pack. He appeared well and...built. Her mouth went dry. The last time she'd seen Shawn, he'd possessed the body of a young man—all gangly arms and legs, not properly filled out. His body now consisted of a seasoned wolf—muscular in all the right places.

"Who is he?" Ashley came up beside her. "He's got the eyes of a predator stalking its prey."

"Uh, he's a friend from home." Better to give a little information than none at all and raise suspicions.

"Is he taken?"

Brienne swallowed a possessive growl. "Yes," she bit out, clipping his order to the turnstile above the counter.

"Damn," Ashley replied. "Does he have a brother?"

Brienne shook her head. "No."

"Boy, what bug crawled up your butt and died?" Ashley, her best friend and member of the Rosewood pack, gave her the stink eye while clipping her order into place next to Brie's.

"Nothing. Everything. I can't talk about it. Do you mind if we switch sections? I'll take yours and you take mine?" She needed to put some distance between her and Shawn. If she didn't, she'd take everything he said at face value. Brie couldn't allow herself to be taken advantage of, or kidnapped and brought to Magnum. *Magnum is dead.* She wished she could believe him.

"Sure, I don't mind. I'll grab his order, too, so you don't have to." Her friend grinned. "Maybe I'll get the down-low on him."

Brienne inclined her head then headed to Ashley's section. If she allowed herself the time to dwell on what could have been, she'd run over to Shawn and ask him to take her home. *Not yet. Soon though. You can call Gee and ask him if what Shawn told you is true.* And potentially give away some tidbit to tell the bastard alpha where she resided? Hell no. She'd wait out Shawn, then when he finally left, she'd move on too. Her wolf howled in outrage at the thought of Shawn walking away without her or vice versa.

Ugh, stop thinking about him. You have work to do. She gave herself a mental slap and approached a couple sitting at one of the tables

For the next five hours, she went from table to

table getting a mini break every so often. She didn't have time to think about anything besides work. Staying on task comforted her. Kept her curiosity at bay. Because she wanted to hear what Shawn came to say. If she allowed herself to trust him, she'd leave her life in Rosewood behind.

Of course, with the idea of actually trusting Shawn came the necessary questions. What if Magnum really had died? Who became alpha? Ryker? She shivered at the thought. The man did all of Magnum's dirty work, including killing whole families because they threatened the sanctity of his pack. No, if Ryker had become alpha, she'd never go home. She'd never call or send letters. She might miss everyone, but she didn't miss them enough to lose her life—selfish as it may seem.

"It's after ten," Ashley said. "He's still there."

Yeah, tenacious was his last name. "He's waiting on me. I promised to talk to him." She placed the salt shaker back on the table then grabbed the pepper shaker. "Did he order anything else?"

"Peach pie." Ashley grinned at her. "How about you go on over and bring it to him, and I'll finish out my section?"

Helpful much? "Uh, I'm not sure. I don't want you getting bogged down." Brie had already handed the last table their ticket. In fact, filling the salt and pepper shakers was the last thing she needed to do. Everything else was set for the next shift.

"It's fine," her friend assured her. "Go on. If he's waited all night, whatever he has to say must be important."

"I don't know," Brie hedged. Having to sit down and listen to Shawn tell her about what had been happening in their pack made her stomach clench. She didn't need to know about any more death. She didn't want to hear about the poor conditions her pack mates and family endured. "I'm not ready to hear what he has to say."

"No time like the present. What's it going to hurt?"

Everything. "If I'm not back in ten minutes, come and get me."

"Sure. But, if you're enjoying yourself or if it looks like it's heating up, I'll leave you to it."

"Deal." Brienne pulled her apron off and took a deep breath. Whatever happened in the next few minutes with Shawn would decide how she proceeded with the rest of her life. *No pressure.*

Chapter Three

"While I appreciate the offer, I must decline," she blurted out, coming to a stop beside him. Not exactly what she meant to say. "Hi, it's good to see you," was more along the lines of what she'd been going for. "I mean, I'm nowhere near done with my shift and I can't allow Ashley to do all of my work for me. It's best if you return home. I'll call you or someone when I'm ready." There, she'd gotten it all out for Shawn, and now he could leave.

Shawn cut his gaze at her as he took a sip of his coffee. "You're playing chess with me, aren't you?" He took the plate with his peach pie out of her hands.

"Excuse me?" She blinked a few times, shocked by his question.

"I sucked at games. I never won." He placed the plate on the table while turning slightly toward her. His cool, light-green eyes assessed her. A sense of nervous awareness slithered down her spine with his obvious perusal. "I was always stuck on strategy," he admitted. "Predictions never allowed me to see the forest for all the tress. I spent the majority of my time trying to figure out what everyone else was doing."

"I don't understand what this has to do with me." She was confused by the tangent he was on.

"I lost because they were making their moves while I tried to be one step ahead. I guess it's what makes me a good tracker. People, even wolves, are creatures of habits and patterns. It's how I can find someone or something." Shawn took a bite of his pie, chewed, and swallowed. "So, tell me, what move you're on, and I'll tell you where I am, then we'll compromise."

"I'm not on any move."

"Sure you are. Sit down already. I'm not going to eat you...yet. I always eat dessert before the main course." He gave her a cheeky grin and pointed to the bench across from him.

Her wolf warred with her. A part of her wanted to stay standing and tell him to fuck off and leave her alone. After what seemed like forever, she relented and took the proffered seat.

"Perfect. Let's throw pretense out the window, okay? You have a set of answers ready to go for every question I'm about to ask you, right?"

Asshole. "When it counts, sure. Doesn't everyone?" The more they played this silly game, the more uncomfortable and agitated she grew.

"I suppose so. It keeps us safe. Keeps us from getting hurt, which is understandable after everything we've been through as a pack. I get your worry. I get you're afraid—"

"I'm not afraid." Her shrill voice made her wince. An, *I-got-you* smirk pulled at the corners of his mouth. "Fine, I'm a little afraid."

"It's normal. I'd be worried there was something wrong with you if you weren't. I spent the first couple of years away from the pack being afraid." He took another sip of coffee then another bite of pie. "It's why I'm here, too."

He knocked her off-kilter, giving her a serious case of whiplash with his statements. "Uh, okay. What happened to you?"

His brows furrowed. "What do you mean?"

"You almost speak in riddles. Just when I think I understand what you're getting at, you switch direction and go off on another tangent. I swear you have a major case of attention deficit disorder, with hyperactive tendencies."

"Are you psychoanalyzing me? Trying to get into my brain?"

"Nope, just making small talk." Brie shrugged. "Trying to guess which rabbit hole I fell down."

"Well in that case," he stated. "I flip subjects for a reason. It keeps you thinking. Keeps you out of your head. Your answers are significantly more reliable and authentic this way."

"So you like confusing me." She nodded. "Interesting."

Shawn shrugged. "Not really. I have one more question for you, Brie."

"Oh? What?" Dread settled like a lead weight.

"Are you willing to listen to what I'm telling you? Actually believe it and not turn me away like I'm some delusional person out to hurt you?"

Brienne thumbed the napkin in front of her, mulling over his questions. "I should say no."

"Okay." He pushed the empty plate away from him then folded his hands. "Can you look me in the eyes and tell me you don't miss Claire and Fern, or your family?"

Shit. No, she couldn't. She missed them every day. She missed the hills. The scents. She missed her friends. Her home. Dammit, she missed it all. However, not enough to give up schooling and return too soon—or deal with their insane alpha. "A little," she hedged, still trying to keep her desires secret.

"I think you're lying. In fact, I'm more than positive you are." He leaned forward. "You're hiding. You have no inclination to return to the hills...yet, anyway." When she didn't refute any of it, Shawn continued. "You're on your tenth move. You're setting up for the kill." He moved an imaginary chess piece into place. "Checkmate. I can see it."

"How?"

"Because, I already have you in a corner."

"You're mighty cocky, Shawn. I don't remember you being this presumptuous before."

"You're deflecting." He flashed her a small grin.

"This is ridiculous. I should have never sat down to talk to you. I should have had you removed by one of Lance's enforcers," she huffed. "Good night, Shawn. Go home." She stood. Brie needed to get out of there before she continued to listen to him. He mesmerized her...or hypnotized her. *Damned confounded man.*

"I get it," he said, stopping her in her tracks. "I think you're staying here and using Magnum as an excuse. You, in some strange way, believe if you go home, you'll be a chew toy for an alpha long since disposed of. It's okay, though. I understand your irrational fear, even if it is rational for you. I commend you on your dedication. It's great.

Nevertheless, you have nothing to fear anymore."

Checkmate.

"Speaking of which, I have a report due next Monday because I'm in school and all." *Liar, liar, pants on fire.* His shocked expression gave her the advantage...finally. "This is supposed to be my week to work on it." She let loose a whopper of a lie. "There is a motel nearby. I'm sure you don't want to go home at this time of night. Not after driving all this way for nothing." She stayed rooted in her spot.

"Don't you dare walk away," he snarled when she finally took a step forward. The commanding timbre of his voice shook her to her core. Her wolf rolled over and exposed her belly. Her heart hammered. Her mouth went dryer than the Mojave. "Not after dropping the school bombshell on me."

"Shawn," she whimpered before licking her lips. "Whatever you were told, I can't do this."

"Funny, Tinks didn't say a thing to me. She gave me a state to start my search. Nothing else."

What? Her stomach dropped, and she went weak-kneed. Gripping the edge of the table hard, she sat. "You tricked me."

"How?"

"You made me assume someone sent you here to Rosewood to make me go home."

"No, I didn't. Your guilty conscience played games with you. Made you jump to conclusions you shouldn't have," he corrected.

Brienne sighed.

"You're bound to go a little bat shit and get paranoid when you've run away and have no clue what's happened in your pack. It's human nature and our wolf nature as well." He shrugged. "We don't like being cornered. It feels like we're being caged."

"You can say that again," she mumbled. "It's not...I mean...I want to go home." She returned to the table and took a seat.

"Not now, though?" he added. "Because of school."

"Right. I can return after the end of the semester." She'd won this round. "I graduate then."

"How about a compromise?" A bit of playfulness colored his tone. "It's a small compromise."

"Nothing, I have a feeling, is small about you or your schemes." She gave him a droll look.

"Perhaps." He gave her a cocky smirk.

"I think I have a headache." She groaned.

Shawn grunted. "Luckily, I've got all night."

"No, please no." She held up her hands, warding him off. "What is your compromise?"

"I want one week in the hills with you," he replied. "Only one."

"If I say no?"

"If you say no, I'll make sure you never have to come home. I'll also make sure Claire understands you're happy, healthy, and fine." He held out his hand.

"Why?" she whispered. "Why would you tell them anything of the sort?"

"Because if you don't or won't give me one week on pack land with you, then I'll know you're serious about not coming home. Plus, the bullshit fairy tale you keep telling about going home at the end of the semester is to make yourself feel better."

"What about Magnum?" she questioned. "How will you deal with him?"

"I told you, he's dead. Drew has taken over the

pack, and things are slowly changing. If you give me the week, I'll prove it."

Maybe Magnum is dead. Did she have the wherewithal to see this for herself? Could she take that leap of faith? "One week?"

"Yep. One."

Brienne mulled it over. The idea of Shawn telling anyone she didn't want to come home and wished they'd leave her alone burned her soul. Her heart lurched at the idea. Her wolf howled in agony. "If you return tomorrow, I'll give you my answer."

Shawn let out a breath and nodded. "Tomorrow. I'll be here at the diner at eight in the morning. I'll also make sure Drew is aware you're coming."

"Because Drew is the new alpha? Why would you tell him anything if I haven't agreed?"

"Call it a sneaky hunch."

Oh great. What have I gotten myself into?

***

Shawn followed Brienne home. Call it being creepy or stalkerish, he didn't care. He needed to make sure she was safe. Trying to talk to her about the pack and what happened since she left was like pulling teeth. He'd expected her to be a little obstinate, but not in total denial. Not paranoid. He snorted. *Yeah, right.* He should have expected nothing and hoped for the best.

When he was satisfied she was safe, he left. He didn't know what surprised him more. Her candor or the skepticism and the downright fear she exuded when she first saw him. All three made it easy for him to talk to her and hard to leave her. Yet, there'd been moments when the sweetest hint of her arousal curled around him, enticing him to take a sip of her sugary nectar.

He glanced in his rearview mirror as the two-story apartment building where Brie lived grew more distant with each tick of the odometer. Part of him wondered if he should have stayed with her—initiated a full-court press. Bind her to him so she'd have to come home.

His gut said give her space.

His wolf demanded he bring his mate home. *Now!*

Shawn had never seen himself as a mate. Never even imagined settling down—despite the certainty of a babe's words, when she'd been six years old.

They'd been a childhood fantasy. A crush. Sure, his wolf might have recognized her. But, did a child's admission mean forever? Shawn didn't have the answer to that particular question. He'd dated a few shifters while he was away but never made the same connection he created with Brienne. *Duh, stupid. She's your mate.*

In theory. Not in practice.

Due to her age, he hadn't tested those waters. Maybe if their pack had been different, he'd have pursued the mating when they were both of age. He wouldn't have left. She might not have either. He also wouldn't be the man he'd become, and perhaps the same could be said for Brie. He, more than likely, wouldn't have helped all those families who'd needed him. She might not have gone to school. Their lives may not have matured them and made them who they were today.

The turnoff for the motel came up fast on the

right side of the road. Shawn followed the small side street and pulled into the driveway. Not too bad. He'd seen worse. The desire to turn around rode him hard. He needed to breathe in her scent. He craved touching her. Holding her. He wanted to mate her. His wolf snarled, desperate to be set free to find his mate. Be damned with the consequences.

Instead, he parked his truck near the entrance then grabbed his bag. The cool nip of late-night air bit at his cheeks as he got out. Not the same as the Black Hills. Not as comforting or as welcoming. He strolled inside the lobby and up to the front desk. After taking his key, he rode the elevator to the third floor then walked the short distance to his room.

He couldn't help thinking about what would happen in the morning. If Brie decided to go with him, how would she react to Los Lobos and the way it looked? Would it scare her? Would she be surprised? Enjoy it? Would it make her stay? Or run away at how much things had changed?

He hoped she'd consider staying. He hoped she'd see the town...the revitalization of the pack, and make the right decision. Of course, he had to admit, when he returned, some people were still a little shaky, and there remained some issues, but, for the most part, things were getting better.

Speaking of happy, Fern would want an update. Shawn pulled his phone out as he stepped inside his room. The door swung close behind him, and he dropped his bag near the bed as he waited for Fern to answer, if she retained a cell signal.

"You called," she exclaimed after two rings. "Did you find her?" The absolute and genuine excitement filling her voice, made him smile.

"I did." He glanced out over the rolling terrain behind the hotel. "I'd like to say this was pure skill, but I had a little help."

"Is she well?" In the background he heard Henry settle in beside her, mumbling about the time.

"She is. You'd be very proud of her."

"Fantastic news. When is she coming home?" Right to the point. He loved his aunt's directness.

"Well, I can't say for sure. I gave her a deal," he replied.

"You're trying my patience, boy," she admonished him. "You made a deal? No more dragging this out. Tell me what is going on."

"Pushy, pushy," he teased then sobered when she growled. "The agreement is simple. Tomorrow morning, I am meeting her at the diner where she works. If she says yes, we'll be home late tomorrow. If she says no, I'll know she honestly doesn't want to come home."

"It's not what we agreed to," his aunt snarled then blew out an exasperated breath. "I need her to come home, Shawn."

"Easy. I don't need Uncle Henry kicking my ass." When she settled down some, he continued, "I have a feeling she'll say yes. She's scared. Worried Magnum is still alive and will harm her or me, if she comes home. I told her she's safe, but she can't reconcile the two fears yet. I believe giving her tonight to think about everything will help her settle herself and see reason. There's more, though."

"Oh?"

"She's in school, and she says she's almost done. Of course, she hasn't told me what she's doing or becoming, but I figure she'll tell me on the way home."

"When will she finish?" Curiosity laced Fern's question.

"The end of the semester is what she's telling me," he replied. "I'm thinking it's not far off though."

"Are you sure?" Eagerness filled his aunt's voice.

"Yes."

"Oh," she gasped. "Oh, this is good news. Very good news!" She clapped her hands together as a giggle bubbled up from her.

"I hope so," he agreed. "I'll find out more in the morning."

"Don't leave me hanging, boy. What else did you find out?"

"She's happy. Lance, the alpha of the Rosewood pack has taken care of her. She has friends and she looks...good." Better than good. She'd worn skin-tight jeans and a fitted shirt with the diner's logo showcasing her generous breasts. His palms itched to touch all of her lush curves while his mouth watered, yearning to taste every inch of her.

"Wow," Fern whispered. "I can't wait to tell Claire."

"You can't." Maybe he'd been a little too quick with his words. "I mean, I'd rather wait to tell Claire until we have a definite answer about coming home for the week."

"Oh." Dejection laced the one syllable word. "I think you're right. Don't want to get anyone's hopes up just to have them dashed again."

"Exactly," he replied. "I think she'll come, though."

"Good. Then we'll have a celebration when she returns." Fern was already getting way ahead of herself. She had a bad habit of doing so, even though she meant well by it. It was one of the things he loved about her, but it also frustrated him. "I'll make sure Drew is there, and Betty. Of course Claire and Joe. Chris. There is much work to do."

"I love you to pieces, Auntie, but I think you need to slow down. Remember, she might say no."

"Nonsense." A cabinet clicked closed. "If you have a feeling she'll return with you then it's official." She brushed off his statement. "I'll make sure there is plenty of food for everyone. Before I go through our family cookbook, is there anything special you want?"

Leave it up to his aunt to forge on. "I'll be happy with whatever you make." He accepted the fact she was excited and nothing would stop the roll she was on. "I know I have been home for a little while, but I thought I'd reiterate how much I missed you while I was gone."

"We missed you, too, Shawn. I'm so glad you came home to us," she sobbed softly. What he wouldn't give to be able to hug her right now.

"All right, you two," Henry growled, taking the phone from Fern. "No more crying and no more emotional crap. My mate hates it when her eyes get puffy."

Shawn laughed. "I'll see you tomorrow."

"With Brienne?" Fern added.

"If she says yes," he replied, then spoke to his uncle. "Don't let her get too crazy with this. I'm not convinced Brie will come with me."

Henry chuckled. "Son, when my mate sets her mind to something, there's no stopping her."

He frowned and nodded. "It's what worries me the most. Letting her down."

Chapter Four

Brienne paced the length of her room. Was she really contemplating going home? Hadn't she promised herself she'd wait? Shawn showing up hadn't played into her wants and needs. He didn't even talk about himself. Rather odd if anyone asked her. In fact, the only tidbits of information she'd gleaned from him left her a bit shell-shocked. Magnum's death and Drew's return.

Did she want to know any more than he told her?

She wouldn't be pacing, even contemplating going home, if she hadn't been the least bit curious. Right?

Shawn's lack of talking intrigued her—not like she'd given him a choice. Sitting across from him, she'd seen the desire in his eyes—the longing to explain everything and the hope. Instead, she'd blocked him at every turn. She spoke little and even listened less. What had she become? Wasn't she the one who wanted to be a therapist and listen to those in need of validation? Wasn't he in need of said validation? Brienne scrubbed her face.

She'd totally and unequivocally rebuffed him and his presence. Sure, she agreed to give him an answer about going to Los Lobos. But she'd only been placating him, right? An answer of no to going home sat on the tip of her tongue, yet she couldn't force the word out. Not even the beginning syllable of the word no. It had seemed simple at the time. *No, Shawn. I don't want to go with you.* But, even as she thought it, the yearning to go home overrode the need to stay away.

Sitting on her bed, Brienne sighed. One night to think about it didn't seem long enough. She glanced around her eight-by-ten bedroom. *You're fooling yourself.* Yeah. One night wasn't long enough. Because she'd realized she'd say yes, the minute he told her to think about it, even though she'd promised herself six more months. Seeing Shawn caused overwhelming homesickness to settle inside her stomach like a lead weight.

"I guess it's time." She needed to pack a bag. She couldn't give him a week. A week would cause her to question everything. No way in hell she'd give up her dreams for her mate. A mate who'd left her all those years ago.

Brienne sighed. This shouldn't be so hard. She shouldn't feel so angry. She needed to put away her claws. Stop gnashing her teeth.

Hard to do after ten years.

Well, you've got to do it or else he'll leave and you'll never be able to go home. Again, she posed the question to herself—do you want to go? *Yes.* More than anything she wanted to go home. Tomorrow she'd embark on a new adventure. Strange as it sounded, it *felt* right. She grabbed her bag out of the closet and began to pack it. As she gathered her things, she grinned. *I'm going home.*

The next morning, she woke early and was ready an hour before Shawn was supposed to arrive at the diner. Dreams of running through the forest being chased by a large, dominant timber wolf woke her several times, breathless and tangled in her sheets. The wolf didn't scare her. In fact, she recognized the wolf. *It's Shawn.* Still, the minute he pounced on her and held her in place, ensnaring her with his unusual-colored eyes, she startled awake. Twisted in her sheets, she lay there covered in sweat. Her heart pounding. Her mind racing. She'd been so close to completing the mating. Two seconds from feeling what it'd be like to have sex with him. Why did she have to wake up?

As she paced the length of her room again, she wondered if she was making a terrible mistake. Did seeing him after so many years cloud her judgment? Make her foolhardy when she should have been stalwart in her convictions? Brienne groaned. With no way of calling him and telling him never mind, the decision was made—partially. However, if she told him no when he arrived at the diner, she'd change her mind just as quickly. Or, she'd spaz out. Lose all ability to string multiple words together in a coherent sentence, and go along with him, because he is, after all, her mate.

Nothing in life should be this hard. Her overnight bag sat by the door staring at her. Her keys on the table called to her. Taunted her. Didn't she tell herself it was only for a week? Her heart understood what her jittery nerves didn't want to admit.

A spark of excitement filled her even as the knots of unsure tension built inside her.

In all honesty, she wanted to see her aunt and uncle. She wanted to see Tinks. She was curious about Drew and how everything had changed.

Had it really changed?

She took one last look around her bedroom as determination filled her. One week. She could do it. She would do it. Picking up her keys and purse, she crossed the room and opened the door. Her adventure started now. She had somewhere to be. She locked up then strolled to her car. No more thinking, no more worrying. She'd made up her mind and now she'd follow through.

After throwing her bag in the back of her car, Brie got in then started it up before she pulled out of her parking spot. A week from now, she'd return. A little bit happier and a little bit more determined to finish up her schooling and go home. As she drove through the sleepy town, she memorized everything, not wanting to forget a stitch of what she'd return to. A week. She could do this.

Brienne pulled into the lot of the diner and parked in her normal spot. A creature of habit, she went through the motions of a regular day. *Nothing new to see here people. Run along.* After getting out of her car, she grabbed her things then walked into the diner.

She paid no attention to who might be there or if anyone saw her. Her sights were set on one man, her mate. *No turning around now.* She took another step forward and bumped into an unmovable wall. Brie stumbled backward until a strong hand gripped her arm, steadying her. "Sorry," she muttered. "Stupid of me not to pay attention. Serves me right for being in a hurry."

"Not a problem." Shawn let her go and stood there, a lazy smile on his face, his curly, blond hair brushing against his forehead. His other hand was tucked in the pocket of his jeans, drawing her attention to his groin. Big mistake. Her breath hitched. The rather large bulge excited her. No, terrified her. *Get yourself together, girl. There is nothing to be afraid of. It's only Shawn.* Not true. He wasn't only Shawn; he was her mate. When his light-green gaze met hers, Brienne's heart skipped a beat. "I'm ready. I want to go home."

Next time add a grunt or two, why don't you? It's like you've regressed to a primitive wolf. Yeah, well, she felt like one right now. Afraid of what might come out of her mouth next, she kept it simple. *At least I didn't say I want to jump your bones. Or take me, I'm yours.*

"Relax," Shawn chuckled. "You're acting like a trapped rabbit trying to find a way out."

"Easy for you to say," she mumbled. "I'm not a rabbit."

"Oh no," he teased.

"Not even a little bit."

He laughed. "You're jumpy," he replied, grabbing her bag. "Is this it?"

Like she didn't have enough? "Yeah. One week."

"Right." He nodded.

"Shawn, don't pull any tricks with me," she stated, following him out of the restaurant.

"I don't play games, sweetheart. It's not my style." He took her hand in his, and warmth bloomed, spreading through her from their contact. She relaxed marginally. "Besides, wolves play more interesting games when they're chasing their mates through the forest."

Her stomach dropped. "Good to know."

They walked through the parking lot in compatible silence after his little announcement. The scent of her nervousness mingled with arousal and excitement. The bite of it grabbed him by the balls and squeezed. "So, when we get to the pack lands, where do you want to go first?" He stopped next to his truck.

"I haven't given it any thought" She bit her bottom lip. "Where do you suggest?"

"Well, I'm not sure either." He placed her bag in the bed of his truck then opened the passenger side door for her. "We've got plenty of time to decide though."

"Seven and a half hours."

"Give or take. We'll stop for lunch, of course." He smirked before closing her in.

"Why didn't you have Lucy pack us a lunch?" she asked as he got in on the driver's side. "If you're doing this, people are waiting for me so we shouldn't dawdle."

"Perhaps." He starting the vehicle. "Buckle up."

He pulled out of the parking lot and headed back the way he'd come, surprised by her statement. In all honesty, he'd prepared himself for her to decline his request. Not like it would have deterred him. He'd return weekend after weekend until she agreed, if he needed to. Call it a dogged determination. Call it whatever, but she wanted to come home. She didn't know how to say it, though.

Each mile they put between themselves and Rosewood, Shawn considered a mini victory. So far she hadn't told him to turn around. *If she does?* He entertained the thought for a minute then mentally shook his head. *Nope, I won't take her home.*

"We didn't talk much yesterday. I thought I'd start then you could tell me about you."

"Okay." She turned in her seat. "Where did you go?"

"Chicago." He wasn't surprised by her directness. "Not the best place, believe me, but it worked in a pinch."

"An urban wolf. Interesting. Didn't it make it hard to shift?"

"Oh, it messed everything up." He nodded. "The smells there are ten times what you'd smell even in Rosewood, let alone Los Lobos. But, I got good at pulling them apart and finding what I was looking for."

"Really?"

"Yep. I worked this missing child case," he started. "The kid ran away from home. A fourteen-year-old who thought she was grown. Anyway, when her mom wasn't looking, I grabbed one of her shirts and took a whiff."

Brienne laughed. "I bet it would have been difficult to explain."

Shawn grinned. "Very. I listened to everything the woman told me about the daughter's friends, contacts. I went through her computer and diary. Nothing came up as suspicious, but kids are sneaky, they can hide whatever they don't want you to see." He cut his gaze toward her. "When someone is unwavering in their need to disappear, they'll go."

"Kind of like us," she whispered.

"A little, sure," he agreed. "I told the mom it might take me a few days, but I'd have answers."

"How quickly did you return?"

"Two days. I'd gotten a list of all her friends. I didn't think she'd gone far. Her scent still lingered in the area. So I followed it, made a show of checking with everyone then found her at the last person's house on the list."

"What happened?" She leaned closer, interest sparking in her gaze.

"I introduced myself, explained the situation and what I'd been sent to do." He still remembered the look on the girl's face when he showed up. The little curly-haired blonde blanched then tried to tell her friend's parents he was lying. "The kid and the friend gave the parents some cock-and-bull story about her being abused and needing a place to hide."

"Wow."

"After assuring the friend's parents nothing of the sort happened or might have happened, I brought the kid home. Then, I made her tell her parents why she'd left and what she told people." He grinned. "I have never seen a set of parents more relieved and furious at the same time."

"I bet. What else did you do?"

"Found cheating spouses. More kids. Anything and everything coming across my desk, I did."

"Didn't you worry about humans finding out about you?" Curiosity lit her words as they turned off the main road and headed for the freeway.

"Nope," he answered truthfully. "I learned when and where I could shift and for how long. In the city, it's hard, sure, but I could drive an hour away and find fields. Nothing like here, but enough space to stretch my legs and not get caught."

"What about other stuff?"

"Sex?" He supposed they'd have to broach the subject at some point.

"Among other things." She shrugged.

"I found other shifters, kept it low-key, but" —he reached for her hand—"I couldn't bring myself to get into any type of romantic or relationship entanglements. Hard to explain I had someone at home."

Her lips thinned and her brows furrowed. "But it didn't stop you from having sex."

"No," he admitted. "I didn't do it often." Like it would make all the difference in the world. "I didn't think I'd return here, either. I thought I'd have to move on. What about you?"

Brienne sighed. "I had a boyfriend my freshman year."

"And?"

"It didn't go very well," she mumbled. "It didn't feel right."

"A function, correct?" He waited for his wolf to snarl and gnash his teeth at the thought of someone else touching her. Instead, his wolf hated the stink of embarrassment tinged with shame and humiliation rolling off of her in thick waves. "There is nothing to feel bad about or be ashamed of. It's normal and a function we all do."

Chapter Five

"**B**oy, you really like to marginalize and minimalize sex," she quipped with a snort.

"It's a talent." He switched lanes so he could merge onto the interstate going west. "I should prepare you...." A slight bit less than a disaster than when he returned, Los Lobos still stood proudly among the Black Hills. Even with Spencer and the destruction he caused, all the work they'd done made a statement. You couldn't break them. "Los Lobos is...well, it's not like it used to be—when we were kids. In fact, in some ways it's better, but it's still bad."

Brienne gasped. "How bad?"

She needed to have the truth. If he expected her to stay, he needed to be up front and not beat around the bush. "When I came home, it looked good-ish. There are a couple of construction places building homes and fixing up buildings." New shops were opening practically every day, even with psycho Spencer wreaking havoc on the town. "Unfortunately, there was a setback this past winter."

"So, it's gone? Town, I mean. The whole place?"

"Some, not all. There was an incident after I returned."

"More? Hasn't everyone been through enough?" Her hand covered her mouth as she shook her head. "What happened?"

"A mate went crazy. Only, I don't think anyone fathomed his status as a mate. He kidnapped Saja, Ryker's ma—"

"Ryker has a mate?" Disbelief laced her tone. "Why was he allowed to stay in the pack? He...he did things Magnum made him—"

"No, he didn't. Ryker did more to protect us than he ever wanted anyone to know. How do you think you got out so easily? Or me?" he asked. "Do you really believe Ryker, if he were as evil as you believe him to be, would let us go?"

"But he...."

"Nope." He grinned.

"Whoa," she murmured. "I guess I should take him off the dick list, huh?"

"Yeah." He laughed. "So she's pregnant to boot. Anyway, Tinks and Tasha led Ryker—"

Brienne stiffened beside him. "What?"

Shawn gave an impatient sigh. "Which part this time?

She blushed. "Sorry. This is all a little overwhelming."

"It's okay. Tinks has become quite the little helper around the pack." He glanced over at her. "Did you know she has a son?"

Her cheeks grew redder and spread down her neck. "Um...."

"You did! I should have guessed." He shook his head.

"If it makes you feel better, I didn't know the gender of the baby. She found the squalling bundle in the middle of the woods, behind her house. The last I heard, no one had any clue who the parents were."

"It's maddening. So much death and destruction. Anyway," he stated, changing the subject. "With Tasha's and Tinks's help, Ryker found Saja before she got hurt then dealt with the crazy wolf."

"Wow," she murmured. "Way to go, Tinks."

"I agree." Shawn threaded his fingers with hers.

For the next few hours, they drove in companionable silence. He hadn't told her everything, nor did she ask. They had plenty of time to talk about things. He was happy to have her beside him, finally.

"I snuck out with Tinks's help," she admitted, breaking the silence. "For a year before I left, I'd go to Hill City and work in one of the diners down there, under the table of course. I'd wash dishes and clean up. The money I made bought me a bus ticket. I chose to go east instead of south or west."

"What are you studying in school?"

"Psychology. I want to be a therapist so I can help the women in the pack. Those who were hurt by Magnum." She shrugged. "It's the least I can do after running away."

"Are you hungry yet? I'm starved." He broke the tension filling the cab of his truck.

Her stomach gave an appreciative growl at his question. "I didn't even eat dinner last night. I was...am so nervous."

"Then we'll grab some lunch. Anything in

particular?" He cocked a brow.

"Right about now, a side of elk or deer would be great." She grinned.

"You're speaking my language," he growled. "We'll go hunting when we get home."

"I'd love to. However, for now, I'd take a burger and fries. Better to eat on the run."

"Makes sense to me." He took the off-ramp. "So, therapy, huh? I think you'll have a valuable service to add to the pack. I think Drew will understand why you left, too. He'll also be happy to have you home."

"Yeah?"

"Of course. Want to hear a good one?"

"Sure, since we're going for broke here."

"Humans can be mates now," he announced.

"No way! Ryker would have killed them."

"Not now."

"I feel like I have missed everything."

Shawn pulled through the drive-thru and ordered them something to eat before getting onto the highway for the last part of their journey. He stared at her out of the corner of his eye every so often gauging how she was handling the news. He caught the thread of excitement she fought hard to contain. He didn't blame her. Going home after everything was a big step. But one in the right direction.

"So, you locate people for a living. What do you do in Los Lobos now?" she asked before popping a fry into her mouth.

"The same. I'm thinking of opening a little business and helping Saja. She writes everyone's history and she's been trying to find others as well."

"Cool." She nodded. "How is Gee?"

"The old bear is still spry and full of it," he laughed. "You missed the knockdown fight outside the bar. Ryker verses Gee."

"No." She turned slightly in her seat and placed her box on the center console.

"Do you remember Kole and Ginger?"

"Of course, she was my best friend when we were younger. How are they?" She grabbed her burger and began to unwrap it.

"They're good. Kole opened a bookstore, and they're running it together."

"Whoa," she said, before taking a bite.

"And Kole has not one, but two mates," he added, grabbing a few fries.

"Serious?"

"Yep." He grinned.

"Amazing." She smiled. "I'm happy for him."

"They dote on him. I swear if he gets a paper cut, one is there to clean it, and the other is there to kiss it better." He gave a wry laugh.

"Well, good for him. They deserve happiness." She took a bite of her burger. "What about Ginger? Does she have a mate?"

"Nope." Shawn frowned. "No one talks about it. But Magnum did things to her and Kole."

"Magnum hurt a lot of people." She placed her burger in the box then wiped her hands on her napkin.

"The Truesdales are back. Along with Kru Hawthorne. Also Chris as well."

"Lily?"

"Yeah. She's working with her brother on the old homestead." The interchange for State Route 14 came up fast and he followed the Y in the road.

"The more I sit here with you, the more excited I get about going home," Brie admitted. "I didn't think I'd feel this sort of anticipation."

"Oh? What did you think you'd feel?"

"Dread."

***

The sun had sunk below the horizon when he pulled off the state highway and onto the rutted and grooved road leading to Los Lobos. Brienne slept peacefully for the last leg of the journey. After her confession of dread, Shawn wasn't sure how to express his own feelings. "I felt the same way" didn't convey his understanding of her words. Sure, he'd had a rough go when he left, but he'd soon found his place within a metropolitan forest of people.

Brienne had left for fear of what a crazed man would do to her. He couldn't imagine how many times she'd looked over her shoulder or stayed awake at night listening to the creaks and groans of an old apartment settling. He hadn't had a chance to thank Lance for keeping her safe, but he would later.

"Brie," he whispered, while touching her leg. "Wake up. We're almost home." Shawn came around the bend in the road and in the distance lay Los Lobos.

"Oh my," she muttered, sitting up in her seat a bit more. "Is this all we have left?"

On the outside, it looked lean and broken down. But they weren't close to the center of town yet. "It'll get better. Remember what I told you?" She nodded. "It gets better."

He continued on, driving by Lobo's Café and Los

Lobos Books and More. "Whoa...." She turned to gaze out the window. "How many businesses are there now?"

"More than a few less than twenty." He shrugged. "But, what's here is staying." They passed the convenience store and a few shops in the process of being rebuilt. "So, where would you like to go first?"

Brienne bit her lip. "I think I should go home first. See my aunt."

"Sounds like a plan." He turned off the main thoroughfare and headed out the dirt road where Claire lived. His aunt and Claire only lived a mile apart.

Several times he wanted to say something...anything. Instead he drove. As the truck ambled down the lane, he took her hand, lending her the strength and courage she needed at the moment. He smelled her anxiety and the thickening blanket of her fear. She swallowed hard, and, out of the corner of his eye, he saw her lip tremble. "Hey now," he crooned. "Everything will be fine. You'll see. She's going to be happy you're home."

"And if she's not?" Brie wiped away her tears as the scent of her shame clung to him.

The hackles on his wolf rose, as he snarled. "Why wouldn't she be?"

She shrugged. "Because I ran away?"

"Well, you're fixing to find out." The door to the house opened and Joe came outside. At least six foot five, and two hundred and forty pounds of brick shit house, he crossed his arms as a curious look filled his face.

"Joe," she cried. "Stop the truck. Stop the truck."

Shawn chuckled. "Let me get a little closer first before you go running after him."

Brienne bounced in her seat. When he finally came to a stop, she jumped out of the truck and ran for the porch. Shawn allowed them their privacy. Brienne leaped into her uncle's arms while her aunt waited, sobbing. Claire's shoulders shook with each soul-shaking cry.

Finally, when Joe let her go, Brie wrapped her arms around Claire. The older wolf nodded in Shawn's direction and mouthed *thank you*. Torn between waiting to stay and appreciating the fact he could spend time with his mate later, Shawn grabbed her bag from the bed of the truck and placed it on the step. Brie turned to him. "Thank you, Shawn."

"My pleasure, Brienne. If you feel up to it tomorrow, would you like to grab lunch with me at Gee's?"

She smiled. "I'd love to have lunch with you."

"Great." Shawn looked to Claire and Joe. "It's better you find out now. Fern is planning something big. I couldn't stop her when I talked to her last night. She's got it in her mind to make this a celebration."

Claire laughed while wiping her eyes. "I wouldn't expect anything less from Fern. We'll be there, whenever this little party of hers happens."

"Great. I'll see you later." He raised his hand in good-bye then started for his truck.

"Wait," Brie called out. Her light footfalls grew closer. He stopped to face her. "Thank you. You were right." She went to her tiptoes and brushed a kiss over his lips.

It took all of his willpower to stand there and not take more. "You're welcome." He pressed his forehead to hers. "I'll see you for lunch tomorrow." He kissed her. "Go on. I have a feeling they have tons of questions for you."

She giggled and nodded. "See you tomorrow."

Chapter Six

The evening went well. Brie spent most of the night catching up with her aunt. Of course she did most of the talking while her aunt forced her to eat. She'd done her fair share of crying as well.

Their conversation went from one topic to the next. Mostly about school, some of it had been about Los Lobos. She didn't want to know about the past. About the pain and suffering they went through. How much everyone lost.

She did want to hear about the changes since Drew took over. The laughter she saw in her aunt's and uncle's eyes when they spoke about the Winter Solstice celebration. Or how every day it seemed like old pack members came home. Yes, there were some bumps in the road. Yes, "perfect," might be a way off, but the idea gave the pack a goal to work toward.

Brienne stared at her reflection in the mirror and sighed. How was she supposed to go home after being here a week? She hadn't been there for even a day yet, and it felt like forever. Did she have to leave?

"Yes, you do," she muttered to herself as she pushed a lock of hair out of her face. "School first, life later." Mating came much later.

"Brie," Claire called out. "Shawn's here, sweetheart."

She scented him the minute the door opened. It happened to be why she stood in the small, dim-lit bathroom. "Coming." She took one more look in the mirror then sighed.

This afternoon she'd break the news to Shawn. She needed to return to Rosewood. She couldn't move home yet. Even if it hurt her soul to leave. Rosewood was her only chance at finishing college. If what she felt and what Shawn explained were true, then they'd always be mates. Whether today or six months from today, she'd be his and he'd be hers.

She stepped into the living room and tripped over her own two feet. Shawn stood before her wearing a pair of slacks and a white button-down dress shirt. The sleeves of his shirt were rolled up, exposing the corded muscles of his forearms. His pants hugged his trim waist. Shawn slicked his unruly curly hair back. His green eyes gleamed with flames of desire...lust...she didn't want to speculate. A sly grin tugged at the corner of his lips. She'd never seen a more beautiful wolf. Staring down at her jeans and shirt, she felt woefully underdressed.

"I should change," she mumbled.

"Why?" He took a step toward her.

"If you have to ask, then I really should change." She turned to escape to her room, however Shawn stopped her.

"You look great. Don't change."

Says the man practically wearing a suit. "It'll

only take me a minute."

"Brie," he muttered. "Don't change."

How could he not want her to change? Her drab appearance compared to his polished.... Shouldn't she fit him? Shouldn't she want to try to look appropriate? Why did she care? Didn't she tell herself not more than five minutes ago, she would be leaving in a week?

"Leave well enough alone, Brie." Joe's booming voice cut through her thoughts. "You look fine."

She nibbled her lip. "I don't know...."

"You're beautiful, Brie." Shawn closed the distance between them. "People won't care what we're wearing. They'll be more interested in seeing you." Her ran his thumb across her cheek and smiled.

"Fine. Did you have to look so scrumptious though?"

Shawn laughed. "I'm trying to impress you. I usually only wear this stuff when I'm meeting a client."

"Oh great."

"It's not so bad." He guided her to the door. "I'll take care of her."

"We know you will, son," Claire said coming up beside them. "Have fun, dear." She kissed Brienne's cheek.

"I will Auntie," she said.

Crisp mountain air sprinkled with the hint of summer flowers filled her senses. The sweet scent wrapped around her like a welcome home hug. She hadn't paid attention to much the night before. Too nervous at the prospect of seeing her family and a dilapidated town, she hadn't taken a moment to breathe in the fresh air of home or explore the places she once used to roam.

In the distance, an owl screeched. Farther away a wolf howled. The longing to run free crashed over her, surprising Brienne with its ferocity. Her wolf brushed against her skin, encouraging her to give over to baser needs. She glanced over at Shawn who stared at her, and saw his wolf reflected in his gaze.

"I'd like to run. Later...after lunch."

"I'll bet you would." Shawn helped her into the truck then came around the front and got in. "I've found a few places to stretch my legs, if you'd like to go there."

"Sure. Everything has changed and I can't find my old trails," Brie admitted.

"From what Fern and Henry told me, some of the trails were allowed to overgrow. It helped Magnum keep a close eye on everyone. So, places you'd have gone before have returned to nature."

Made sense to her. She actually liked the idea.

"Then we'll find new ones, together."

"Yes we will."

"Okay. Burger and beer?"

"Perfect."

***

Shawn led her into Gee's and picked a table near the bar. The place was packed. Good music and laughter filled the air, but it abruptly stopped when Brienne stepped into the space. All eyes were on his mate. Not like he blamed them. Her jeans molded her slim figure, showcasing her ass. Jesus, she teased him like no other female or shifter could.

Paul came over and gave Brie a warm smile then scrawled something on his pad. He laid the paper on the table in front of Brienne then waited. *Long time no see, stranger. When did you get home?*

She glanced up. "Last night."

"I brought her home. She's had more than enough time to hide." He winked at Brie who frowned at him.

Paul scribbled another note for them. *I agree. I'm glad you're home, Brienne. What can I get for you guys?*

The omega took their order and dashed off to the kitchen. Shawn placed his hand in hers then ran his thumb over the sensitive skin between her thumb and forefinger. "So, about this run."

"Yes." Her pulse quickened.

"How far do you want to go?"

She shrugged. "I want to escape. I want to be a wolf and just enjoy myself."

Shawn inclined his head. "I understand. Did you run much while in Rosewood?"

"Sometimes. I mean school and work kept me busy."

"Hmm, then you have some making up to do."

"I guess so."

Paul brought them their lunch and for a while, they sat in amicable silence. The chatter around the bar seemed to settle on the most recent activity within the pack. The death of several pack mates along with the excitement of new members soon to be born. If Brie paid attention, she didn't give any outward indications, which threw him off.

Didn't she want to be a part of what they were

talking about? Wasn't she curious about the mates expecting babies? Didn't women go insane over stuff like this? "Hey."

"Huh?" She startled "Sorry."

"Don't think so hard," he teased. "Are you almost done?"

"Are you in a hurry?"

"To run with you? Hell yeah, I am." He wiped his mouth with a napkin. "I've been ready since I set foot in the diner."

"Well, who am I to hold this up any longer?" She slid her plate forward then pushed out of her chair. Standing, she waved at Gee, who nodded in return. "Let's go."

Shawn dropped a few bills on the table to cover their lunch and a tip for Paul before taking her hand and leading her out of the bar. From the corner of the building he could hear the sounds of a couple moaning. "Well they have the right idea," he muttered.

"Oh God, are they...."

"Fucking? Yep. Seems to be a new past time for people around here. Want to join them?" He cocked a brow only half-serious about his proposal.

"Banging against a wooden wall which could embed splinters into my ass, is not the makings of a good time."

"Who said anything about getting any splinters?" He wiggled his brows.

Brie broke away from him and laughed. "You're incorrigible."

"Can't blame a wolf for trying." He shrugged, tugging her into his arms. "Especially when I'm with one of the most beautiful wolves I've ever seen."

"I bet you say the same to all the women you try to bed."

"Never. I don't say shit I don't mean." He cupped her cheek, tipping her face up to him. "You are the most beautiful woman I have ever had the pleasure of meeting." He pressed his lips to hers then licked the seam of her lips and pressed forward, tangling his tongue with hers.

Brienne moaned, and he took advantage, deepening the kiss. Before he'd arrived at Claire's to pick her up he'd promised himself he'd play it cool, but the longer he spent near her, the more he wanted her. Her soft, subtle scent made him salivate most times and left him aching for her the rest of the time. Having her near for even a short period of time made it impossible to stay away or allow her to leave him. He'd have to figure out a way to fix this. To make her want to stay with him.

Shawn pulled away. "You're dangerous, little Brie."

"I'm not so little anymore," she whispered then took a deep breath and let it out slowly.

"No, you're not," he growled in agreement.

After helping her into the truck, Shawn got in beside her and started it up. They drove the short distance to the hills where he liked to run. Beside him, Brie gazed out at the trail. Sometimes he wished he could read people's minds like a few of the other wolves could. It would help him with trying to understand what went on in her head. "Ready?" He popped his door open.

"Yes."

Shawn had the ability to shift with or without his clothes on, and for a second he wondered what was appropriate in this situation. However, before he could ask, he caught a glimpse of Brienne taking off her clothes. His mouth went dry. His heart stuttered before settling into a rapid pace. His groin tightened as all the blood his overactive heart pumped shot south. *Holy shit.*

He began unbuttoning his shirt and realized rather quickly his hands shook. He'd never seen his mate naked before. Sure, he fantasied about it—in great detail sometimes, yet fantasy and reality were two different things. Plus, his fantasies weren't anywhere close to the real thing. *Get hold of yourself.*

The air around him snapped with electricity, raising the hairs on his arms. It called to his wolf, demanding he give over to the change. Shawn removed his shoes and socks before pulling off his pants and welcomed his wolf, embracing it as they melded into his true form. Shawn lifted his nose and scented Brie. Her light, sweet scent tempted him. Called to him. He trotted over to where she waited by the lip of the trail. After rubbing against her in greeting, he took off into the woods, Brienne hot on his heels.

Chapter Seven

They zigzagged through the trees and jumped over rocks as they went deeper into the hills. A couple of times, Brie nipped playfully at his legs before taking off again, going deeper into the thicket. He chased after her, allowing her to believe she had the advantage. Then, when she least expected it, he cut off her path, sending them tumbling down a small incline. She landed on top of him, mirth filling her eyes as she lowered her head to nibble on his neck.

Brie's sleek body rubbed against his, imprinting her scent on him, claiming him. Shawn silently howled in triumph. Her mouth might say one thing, but her wolf said another. Excitement filled her glowing blue eyes as she leapt off him and took off deeper into the shrubbery of the forest floor.

Shawn chased her. The worries of the day, hell, the coming week, didn't seem important right now. As a wolf, all he cared about was the she-wolf determined to play hide-and-seek with him. He shot through the underbrush, hot on her heels, coming to the clearing then stopped and glanced around. *Empty.* He cocked his head, listening for any sign of her. When he didn't hear her, he crept through the area, ready for her to jump out at him.

Leaves to his left rustled and a twig snapped. Lifting his head, Shawn took a deep breath. The gamey scent of deer twined with the scent of his Brienne. He took a step toward the sound then bounded backward as the deer and Brie lunged from the brush and trampled through the clearing. She yipped and continued chasing the animal, forcing him to keep up.

Instead of following, he ran parallel to her, keeping her to his right. They worked together as a team and when they came to the lip of the trail, he went in for the kill. The deer, an eight-point buck, reared up at him and lowered his antlers. Shawn dodged the buck's head and went for his neck. Brienne attacked the legs, trying to drop the beast to the ground.

The animal had spirit, fighting them every inch of the way. Shawn wrapped his jaws around the neck and clamped off its airway, taking the ability to breathe away. The buck continued to jerk and thrash, trying to dislodge him. Instead of losing his grip, Shawn increased the pressure of his jaws. Wide brown eyes gazed up into his as the buck lost his battle. The animal kicked one last time then went limp. He released the buck's neck and stepped away. Brie did the same.

When the animal didn't move, he shifted. Brie did the same then jumped into his arms and laughed. "Holy cow. That was amazing. Did you see me? I mean wow." Her body vibrated with energy.

He chuckled. "I did. You were amazing." He kissed her.

She clung to him, the blunt tips of her nails digging into his shoulders as she wrapped her legs around his waist. Snaps of electricity crackled across his flesh, as he slanted his mouth, deepening the kiss. All thoughts of taking it slow, building up this connection between them, fled the minute she whimpered against his lips. Brienne rubbed her slick folds across his steely erection, tempting him beyond sanity. He should stop this madness. Breathe. Instead, Shawn laid her out on the hood of his truck. She trembled in his hold. He waited—wanting this from the minute he saw her at Lucy's.

Settling between her parted legs, he gazed up her willowy figure and swallowed a desire-filled groan. "Fucking perfect," he growled then scored his nail up her outer thighs and gripped her hips. "Do you understand how much I crave you?"

"Shawn," she murmured. Her dazed, blue eyes fluttered shut as she arched to him.

"Do you?"

"Yes. Because I've waited my whole life for you."

Finally, the walls were down between them. "Do you trust me?"

Brie licked her lips and writhed against him. "Yes. Please."

"Shh." He cupped her cheek. "I've got you."

Shawn ran the pad of his thumb across her bottom lip and she opened to him, drawing the tip into her mouth. The sensation shot straight to his dick, leaving him light-headed. She nipped the appendage before laving away the sting with her tongue. *Minx.* Removing his finger, he lowered his hand and swiped her nipple. The bud puckered under his touch and she moaned. "Why are you going slow?"

"Why do you want me to go fast?" He nibbled her side. "I want to savor this."

"But...." Her breath left her in a whoosh when he circled her navel with his tongue.

"I'm listening." He grinned against her flesh. Placing a kiss to her mons, he nuzzled her clit and inhaled the musky scent of her arousal.

"Shouldn't we be fucking?"

Shawn shook his head then licked her slit. The heady taste jacked up the ache in his balls. "Nope."

"No?" she squealed as he drew her clit between his lips and sucked.

"No." Shawn spread her thighs and settled between them, prepared to spend all day there if he chose. He licked the length of her slit before opening her to his perusal. Her pussy glistened with a mixture of his saliva and her juices. Her clit throbbed and he lapped at the hard ball of nerves once more. Shit, he could feast on her for hours before he got inside her.

Brienne ran her fingers through his hair and pulled his mouth closer. *There you go, babe.* He moaned against her flesh. Her sweet whimpers filled the still air, and his wolf puffed up his chest in pride. He gave her pleasure. No one else.

"Shawn."

He filled her with his tongue and mimicked the same rhythm he'd follow when he finally got balls deep inside her.

He placed one last kiss over her sex and stood up. "This isn't going to be fast. This is a mating, Brie. If you don't want it, you'd better say something now."

Silence prevailed. The seconds ticked by at an excruciatingly slow pace before she nodded. "I'm ready. It's time."

"Thank fuck." He kissed a path up her body as he fit his tip at her entrance. Drawing her nipple into his mouth, Shawn pushed forward. Her muscles rippled around him and Shawn clenched his jaw. The tight, searing heat of her wet pussy threatened to unman him. "Holy shit."

She rolled her hips, taking him into her a little at a time. He wanted to fuck like she'd requested, but it'd be all over before they began. Holding her still, he retreated and surged forward. Her muscles quivered, relaxing around him, easing his forward progression. With each inch he gained, his body heated, and the sound his heartbeat thundered like a herd of wild mustangs in his ears.

Imagination wasn't as good as the real deal.

Brie cried out. *Oh my God.* Shawn meant to kill her. After the run and taking down the deer, the overwhelming need to mate rushed through her. To claim the man she'd yearned for since she recognized him at the age of six scared the crap out of her. A little over twenty-four hours ago, she'd made the decision to go with Shawn but not stay. Now, she didn't think she could walk away from him.

He drew in a ragged breath.

She'd wear his mark in more than one way before the afternoon ended. The death grip on her hips would leave bruises. In one long thrust, he filled her completely, touching her in places no man ever reached. She arched off the hood of his truck, her mouth open on a silent scream. Zaps of electricity snapped along her skin. She tingled from head to toe.

The connection between them built by the second, forming unbreakable bonds. His low growl of arousal turned her on even more. Her pussy went slick around him. Her heart hammered. Shawn lifted her leg and wrapped it around his waist, shifting his position. He surged forward again, and the change of the angle increased the pressure of his groin against her clit.

Fire raced through her veins. Pleasure coiled low in her belly. He'd been serious about the whole claiming her thing. She felt him everywhere. His big body bracketed her. His breath fanned out over her breasts as he dipped his head and sucked her nipple into his mouth. He swirled his tongue around her peak and she swore she felt it all the way down to her clit, like an invisible tether between the two. "Oh God."

"So fucking wet and tight," he snarled, biting the curve of her breast. Her pussy spasmed around him and she groaned. "I've got what you need, sweetheart. We'll get there."

She growled, grabbing his ass. The erotic sensations shooting through her left her reeling. Brie blinked, stunned by the way her body responded to Shawn's. "I need more."

Shawn pulled out and helped her down. "I've got you," he murmured in her ear before turning her around. His palm slid down her spine. "Bend forward." He widened her stance and guided her toward the truck. "Hold on."

He filled her in one stroke, and she screamed. Her pussy contracted and released around him as she exploded. The orgasm ripped her apart while her mate put her back together. He pressed his forehead between her shoulder blades and grunted with each shift of his hips. With each thrust he sounded more like a wolf than a man.

Her wolf preened. "More."

"Hell yeah," he growled. "I'm always going to give you more." His arm wrapped around her middle, pulling her to him. He slid his palm down between her legs. "You're mine, Brienne. Say it."

"I'm yours." She'd always been his.

"Damn right you are." His index finger brushed over her clit.

Her mind shut down. Their slick bodies moved together while he continued to work the bundle of nerves between her thighs. He drew out her desire, letting it burn through her. A few months ago—hell, even a few days ago, the thought of Shawn mating her would have made her run far away. Now, she wanted him. "Mark me, mate."

Shawn groaned. "You sure do have a way with words."

"It's the truth. Mark me."

"What about everything you said before?"

"Please," she implored.

"Fuck yes." He flicked her clit and nuzzled her neck. "You should know this will always be intense for us. I plan on spending the rest of my life watching you get off on my dick."

Brienne shuddered.

"Damn, little Brie. You've got the sweetest pussy." He slammed into her. "Fuck." He ran his tongue up the side of her throat and drew the lobe of her ear into his mouth. "Come," he whispered, while adding pressure to her clit, rubbing in small circles.

She sucked in a breath. A howl of completion fell from her as her release rushed through her. Shawn's pace became erratic. His grunts and growls only served to turn her on even more and pushed her headlong into another climax. The prick of pain at her neck added to the sensations rolling through her. Behind her, Shawn shoved into her one last time and stilled. His long low groan accompanied the feel of him pulsing within her.

Brie sagged.

Shawn tightened his hold of her, cradling her against him. "I should have made sure before we did this...."

"I'm okay." She tried to catch her breath. "We're good."

"Oh, we're better than good," he chuckled. "God, Brie."

"I know," she answered. "I feel it, too."

He pulled out then turned her so she faced him. "This will work out. I promise. I don't care if I have to go with you to Minnesota until school is over."

She nodded. "We'll talk about it later." She shivered. The cool air of the coming evening caused goose bumps to form on sweat-slicked skin. "I think we should get dressed before we freeze out here."

Shawn gave her a sly smirk. "I've got a way to keep us warm."

Brie snorted. "I've created a monster."

"I think that's my line." He palmed her ass then pulled her closer. "I mean it. You're mine. I go where you go, and vice versa." He kissed her and lingered for a moment. Patting her ass, he took a step away. "Come on, we need to get this deer in the truck and get you home, too. Don't need your aunt worrying about you."

"Oh, I am sure she's gathered exactly what I'm doing," she murmured, grabbing her clothes off the seat of his truck.

Chapter Eight

A fter they dressed, they picked up the deer and slid it into the bed of the truck. He closed the tailgate while Brie climbed into the pickup. The afternoon went even better than he'd expected. Not only did he break down the walls surrounding his mate, he'd taken the final step of binding her to him. He meant every word. He'd follow her to Minnesota if need be. He'd contemplated it the night before. Drew would understand as well. Hell, the guy, in Shawn's estimation, would follow Betty into the depths of hell, without question.

Plus, his job didn't require a permanent address. *Have phone will travel.* Once Brie finished school, they'd return to the hills and go from there. She'd needed a little office for her therapy sessions, and he'd work out of the house he'd contemplated building a few months ago. However, it could all wait for now. "You're awful quiet over there."

She slid her gaze toward him. "I'm digesting it all, I think. Trying to fit all the pieces together so

I...we can form a plan."

"I understand. I'm doing the same. How about I pick you up for breakfast in the morning?"

"You're not forcing me or—or making me stay with you?"

He chuckled at her confusion. "No. It'll be part of what we talk about tomorrow. I want to take my time with you, Brie. Today's been...." He blew out a breath. "Incredible. Special. More than I expected."

"But?"

"No buts. I want this perfect. I want us both to work on a plan together and even if we fuck all night, I still only have five days to convince you to stay."

"I thought you said you'd go with me." She pulled her hand away and he gripped her wrist.

"I did and I would."

"Okay," she murmured.

Shawn snorted. "Do you really think us leaving together is the only shit we need to sort out?"

"Well." She shrugged. "I thought we're mates now so what one does the other does."

"The idea is a little selfish, isn't it?"

"I suppose."

Shawn turned off the main road through town and headed for Claire's house. "I'm not going anywhere, Brienne. I think you're still wound tight about being here. I think you want to hurry everything up so you can blow this place."

He eased the truck around the rear of Claire's house and honked the horn. Joe appeared at the entryway of the house moments later. The soft light from the fireplace cast long shadows on the wall behind him. Shawn parked the vehicle then got out. If Brie didn't think he craved having her next to him, she'd be dead wrong. He did. But, he didn't want her to be there because he mated her. He needed her to be there with the pack, in every way. Mind, body, and soul. If there were any lingering doubts about her visit, or even about going home, she needed time to work through them—without his interfering.

Shawn motioned for the older man to meet him at the tailgate of the truck.

"This better be good, son." Joe stopped next to Shawn.

"It is." He lowered the tailgate on the truck and pointed to the deer. "Your niece had a little fun today. I thought we could get it hung so we could clean it."

"Son of a b—" Joe peered over his shoulder at the house where Claire stood. "Brienne didn't go get herself hurt, did she?"

"No." Well, not in the sense Joe spoke about. "We're fine. I killed him, she helped."

"There's enough meat to feed us for a while. He's got to be upwards of two hundred and fifty pounds." Joe lifted the head of the beast, turning it to and fro. "Rack is good...healthy."

"Strong, too," Shawn added. "I want the buckskin."

"Figured you would."

"Great. I'll get Brie situated inside then help you unload this guy."

Joe nodded as he stepped around the man and headed to the passenger side of the truck. Inside, Brie sat, staring at her hands. *Way to ruin the day, asshole. Your mate wants you. Take what's yours.* Shawn growled, fisting his hands. He needed to get himself under control before he did something stupid.

He rapped his knuckles on the window. Brie glanced up then popped the door open. "Only tonight," he whispered, brushing his lips over her temple. "Tomorrow, you'll thank me." He took her hand and guided her out of the truck then leaned in and breathed in her scent. "My mark looks good on you. I can't wait to do it again."

"Shawn," she whimpered. "One night."

"Yes. I expect you to have a plan in the morning." He led her over to the porch where Claire waited for them. "Have a good night, little Brie."

"You, too."

"Oh, and don't forget. We have a party to crash tomorrow."

His little mate turned around. "Yes, we do. Who's going to be at this party?"

"Everyone, dear," Claire answered before he could, laying her hands on her niece's shoulders. "It'll be fun. Fern's been working on this since she learned Shawn found you."

"I suppose everyone includes Ryker?"

"Of course, sweetheart. He's part of this pack, too." Her aunt huffed out a breath. "It seems you and I need to continue our conversation from this morning." She gave Brie a disapproving look. "March, young lady. You're going to listen to me, this time. Good night, Shawn. Thank you for the meat. We appreciate it. In fact, we'll use some of it tomorrow."

"You're welcome." He waited for Claire and Brienne to walk into the house before joining Joe at the truck.

"So, you went and did it," the elder wolf stated.

"Yeah, suppose I did." He gripped the head of the deer while Joe grabbed the rear. "I didn't plan on it happening this way, however I'm figuring out pretty quick, plans don't always go right around here."

"Nope," Joe agreed as they lifted the beast. "Never do."

"I'm going to do everything in my power to keep her here." Shawn strode toward the rack with Joe.

"I know you will," he agreed.

"Why do I have the feeling you're about to whoop my ass?"

Joe chuckled. "Guilty conscience?" They laid the deer under the cleaning rack then released the pulley, lowering the hind leg hooks.

"No." Shawn hooked each leg then began to lift it into place. "I don't regret a moment of today." A little lie. He wished their conversation on the way to the house had gone a little better. "I hope everything goes well tomorrow."

"It will."

"You seem pretty sure of it." He glanced over at the older wolf.

"The girl has been head over heels in love with you since you guys were kids. She's a little skittish right now. Can't say I blame her."

No neither could Shawn. "You're right."

Joe grunted. "Grab my kit. It's over by my butcher table. I'll grab the burn can. We're going to be here for a while."

***

"I thought we were going to Fern's house," she said, as they pulled into Gee's parking lot.

"Last minute change of plans. Seems my aunt, even though I told her not to, got a little carried away." Shawn shut off the truck and turned toward Brie. "Don't worry. Everyone in there will be happy to see you."

"Of course." She took a shaky breath. "It's not like we all haven't come home a time or two, right?"

"Right? It'll be fun."

"Sure." She didn't believe him. At some point, someone—namely Ryker, would ask why she hadn't seen Drew or Magnum or whoever, and she'd have to explain she wasn't sure she'd stay. The conversation about Shawn following her to Rosewood played through her mind all night and made sleep near impossible.

Did she want Shawn giving up his family again for another six months so she could finish school? Didn't it make her selfish to even consider his offer? As much as she liked it in the Hills, she didn't want to give up her dream either. If only she had more time to reconcile her wants and needs. It'd make this whole situation easier to deal with.

Brie got out of the truck and followed Shawn to the entrance. "Remember, we're here to have fun." He slipped his hand into hers and gave it a squeeze.

"Right. Fun." She took a deep, settling breath then stepped over the threshold of the bar. The noise level alone made her want to take a step outside and runaway. Music blared through the speakers as people talked and laughed, seemingly unconcerned by her entrance.

"You're here!" Over the roar of music and chatter, Fern pushed through the throng of people and stopped in front of Brienne. "I was told you might not show up." She gave Brie a disapproving look. "I knew I could count on my nephew, though."

Fern hugged her tight then led her over to the tables beyond the bar. "We've been waiting for you."

Waiting? She thought the plan was to show up at seven. Wasn't it what Shawn told her? She glared at the man beside her for being late then stopped dead in her tracks when she saw Ryker and Drew at the table. "Uh."

"It's about time you showed up. Drew eased out of his chair. "I thought I'd have to hunt you down just to speak with you."

"Well, you see, I—"

"You've been detained," Ryker grunted. "We know."

Why did the enforcer rankle her nerves? Her hackles rose. Her body tensed. "I didn't realize in a free pack, I'm required to report in," she snarled. Beside her, Shawn gripped her wrist. "What?"

"Calm down. No one is going to hurt you here," he whispered. "We're here to have fun."

Ryker cocked a brow at her while the dark-haired woman next to him grinned. "Still prideful."

"You're damn right! I'll always be. So, if you think you're going to beat it—"

"Damn, Shawn, didn't you explain anything to her?" Drew's voice cut through the din of music and the sound of her racing heart.

Shawn chuckled. "I did. She's stubborn. I don't think she believed a word I told her until she saw you. Ryker, on the other hand...."

"*La muerte negro,*" another woman farther down the table added. "I'm Gabby. This is Kru, my mate."

Human. The woman beside Ryker was the same. Kole sat between two hulking men. *Another human.*

Stunned, she blinked a few times and could've sworn Ryker smirked. But it didn't make any sense since Ryker didn't smirk.

"I think your mate is figuring it out," Drew quipped as he sat down.

"I believe you're right," Shawn laughed.

Bewildered, Brie all but collapsed in the chair Shawn pulled out for her. She stared around the long table setup just for them. She wanted to pinch herself because all of this was nothing more than a dream. *And if it's not?*

"So, Claire and Fern have told me you are in school," Drew stated. "What are you studying?"

She licked her lips, trying to find her balance while sitting at a table filled with people she'd hoped to see again. "Psychology. Therapy, to be exact. I have six months left and I'll obtain my master's degree."

"All while under Lance's protection?" Drew questioned.

Brie went still. Her body became rigid with fear. Did Shawn tell them about Lance? "Yes." She couldn't lie.

"Relax," Drew supplied. "This isn't an interrogation. Shawn told us of the Rosewood alpha. I've talked to him as well. Sounds like Lucy is missing her best employee and Amber is missing her best friend. However, they're happy you're home."

"Yeah, well." She shrugged. "I couldn't very well stay here before."

Drew gave a solemn nod. "I agree. I've seen what happens when you leave and when you stay. I'm hoping you'll stay, now, though, Brienne. The pack will and does need someone like you and your talents." He took a sip of his beer. "There's a college about an hour and a half north of here. Black Hills College, to be exact. I'm sure you could transfer in and not miss a beat."

"What?" She didn't believe she heard him correctly. Transfer schools?

"A little presumptuous of me," Drew replied.

"I need something to drink," she muttered. "This is a lot to take in."

"My dear," Fern began. "You left us all when you were a child. Your mind is still running when it should be slowing down and enjoying the view. There is no point in trying to get away any longer. You belong here with your family and your pack."

Damn it. Why did everyone have to be so nice and understanding? Why did Ryker have to smirk at her? Why...why did she come home? *Because it's time and you wanted to.* Brie sighed. She had the strength to do anything she put her mind to, but walking away from her family again, she couldn't do it. "I'll look into it tomorrow, Alpha."

"Drew. Call me Drew."

"Drew." She inclined her head. She glanced over at Ryker. "Would you kindly stop smirking at me? You're freaking me out."

Ryker smiled as everyone at the table laughed. The smile did nothing to smooth out the rough planes of his face nor bring the intimidation factor down. Yep, the man, she figured, would always scare the shit out of her.

With the party in full swing, her pack mates greeted her with open arms. Ginger, one of the people she wished she could see, was nowhere to be found. Tinks, either. She asked a few people if they'd seen her friends, and they all shook their heads. Kole stood near Miss Fern and her aunt. His mates surrounded them and made an imposing duo. Most people ignored the dominant way they protected their mate, but she saw it right off the bat.

She strolled up behind them and cleared her throat. "Excuse me? I don't mean to intrude, but have you seen Ginger anywhere around here?"

Kole frowned. "She's keeping to herself lately."

"She's being petulant," Fern remarked.

Jasper or she thought his name was Jasper, shook his head. "She's lonely and afraid, I think."

"Why?" She was equal parts curious and concerned for her best friend.

"Well, it's only gotten worse since Kole mated us."

Next to him, Max snarled. The last time she saw him, she'd been a young girl and he'd been...a mountain. "She's hiding. It's as clear to me as the night is black."

"Okay, so afraid and hiding." Brie nodded. "She must not like the change going on in her own family. Or, maybe she does like the change and doesn't find herself worthy to have the same?"

"Haven't even set up a practice and you're already at work." Ero sauntered up next to her.

Brie laughed. "I'm worried is all." She turned her attention to Kole. "The bookstore is yours, correct?" He nodded. "I'll be there tomorrow to talk with Ginger."

"Okay." He smiled. "I think you're right, Brie. She is afraid she's not worthy. The things she endured. She's punishing herself. Kind of like you're doing, too." Kole took his mates' hands and walked over to the bar.

"Well, leave it to Kole to say something profound and walk away," she murmured. "When did he become a talker?"

"Since he mated those two." Ero pointed to Max and Jasper. "They've brought him out of his self-imposed solitude."

"I'm glad."

Shawn's arms wrapped around her middle from behind, and all the nervous energy rushing through her, eased. "Ero."

"Shawn."

"Having fun, little Brie?" Her mate nuzzled her neck.

"I am. More than I thought I would." She faced him. "Did you do this in hopes I'd stay?"

Shawn snorted. "I didn't plan any of this. In fact," he chuckled, "I tried to stop it before it got to this point, but my aunt would have none of it."

"Good answer." She grinned. "I think it's time you took me home."

"Is it now?" He brushed his lips over hers.

"Yes."

"And miss the party?" He raised a brow.

"I thought we'd continue it on our own, mate." She nipped his bottom lip.

"I like the way you think." He grinned. "Let's go."

Chapter Nine

B rienne woke early the next morning curled in Shawn's arms. Last night's post-party activities still hummed through her veins. She stared up at her sleeping mate and studied his features. When had they both grown older? Some of his boyish good looks were still there, but a ruggedness she hadn't expected enhanced his features.

Could she really leave him after everything they'd experienced the last few days? Could she also ask him to leave his family behind? No, she couldn't. So, what did she do from here on out? Drew told her she could go to school an hour from there, but would her school transfer everything for her? The only stupid question was one not voiced.

For now, she untangled herself from Shawn's arms and hurried to the bathroom. She made a promise to Kole. She'd go see Ginger. Then she'd find Tinks. The two people she wished she'd seen the night before didn't show up, and though she understood Ginger's issue, she didn't understand

Tinks.

Ten years is a long time to keep running. She turned on the shower and let the water warm. If she got to the root of the matter, she'd been scared. Scared when she left. Scared when she'd been found. After last night she didn't think she had anything to worry about, obviously Magnum died, and things were better...even if the town itself didn't appear so.

Brienne climbed into the tub and allowed the warm water to cascade down around her. She needed to think. Scrap her old plan and come up with a new one. She turned to face the wall and dipped her head to wet her hair. A day. She needed one day to make the calls necessary to find out if she'd be able to transfer schools.

The click of the door opening surprised her. "What are you doing up so early?" Shawn's gravelly voice slid down her spine and pooled low in her belly as he wrapped his arms around her middle.

"I promised Kole I'd go see Ginger this morning." She playfully shifted her hips.

"And you weren't going to tell me?" He pushed her hair from her shoulder then nibbled on the mark he'd left two nights ago.

"I planned on telling you. After I showered and made some coffee for us. I have a feeling today is going to be a long day for the both of us."

"Yeah, I believe you're right. Word got out about what I do. I have several requests for help." He slid his palm up her belly and brushed the sensitive tip of her nipple with the pad of his thumb. "No pressure here, but I could get used to this."

"Showering with me in the morning?" She sighed, and pressed back against his chest.

"No, the intimacy," he replied, still teasing her with his fingertips. "A quiet conversation no one else can hear."

"This is more than a quiet conversation," she whispered. Her eyes fluttered shut and her breath hitched when he rolled her nipple between his fingers.

"Perhaps." He rotated her to face him and cupped her cheek. "But, then again, all things begin with some sort of discussion." He kissed the tip of her nose. "And, as much as I want to continue this, you have plans."

Brie frowned. "True."

"Run with me tonight?" He brushed his lips over hers.

She nodded. "Okay."

Shawn kissed her. He pulled her body flush to his. The hard length of his erection pressed against her hip. "Finish your shower, little Brie. I'll make us breakfast and coffee." He patted her ass then stepped from the shower.

"I really wanted you to scrub my back," she mumbled at his retreating form. His rumbled laugh made her grin.

Once she finished with her shower, and dressed, she joined him in the kitchen. The scent of bacon wafted in the air along with potatoes and onions. He wore only the jeans from last night, the top button open, allowing them to ride low on his lean hips. Her mouth watered. He tempted her without even trying. On the table sat a cup of coffee and a couple of pieces of toast.

"Do you remember how to get to Tinks's house?" he asked, plating up their breakfast. "Would you like to use my truck?"

"Yes, I remember, and I'd love to, but how will you get around?" She took a bite of toast then a sip of coffee.

"Let me worry about getting around." He walked to the table. "I have my ways."

She eyed him speculatively. "Fine, I'll use your truck." She took a bite of her breakfast and moaned. "It's really good. How about I drive you where you need to be first then I'll go see Ginger?"

"Sure. Finish eating, and I'll get ready to go."

"Aren't you going to eat?"

"I have something better to *eat* later." He winked then downed his coffee.

***

"Hello," Brie called out. The bells over the door jingled as she closed it behind her. "Ginger?"

The cute little bookstore didn't surprise her one bit. Between her friend and Kole, they'd come up with a way to include everyone. She drifted over to the children's nook, taking in all the small details. Tinks had created the mural on the wall. Her flare for the mystical added to the whimsical feeling of the space. A fairy sat on a toadstool, a wolf to her right, and a butterfly to her left.

"Sorry, I was in the storage room separating books." Ginger placed a couple of books on the counter behind the register. "Can I help you?"

Brienne turned around and grinned. "Hi." Her friend's eyes widened. "I didn't see you last night at Gee's, so I thought I'd stop by."

"Brie," Ginger whispered. "Oh wow." She took a

step forward. "I didn't...."

"It's okay. Big crowds aren't my thing either. I love what you've done here."

"Kole and his mates have done the majority of it." Ginger pushed a lock of hair behind her ear. "Want some tea? I could use a snack."

"Sure." She grinned. "I can't believe Kole mated with Max and Jasper. A human? I never thought...."

"Yeah, neither did I. But they're happy."

"What about you?"

"Me?" Ginger shrugged. "Does it matter?"

"Yeah, it does."

Ginger shook her head. "There are some things I can't change. I'm not mating material and quite frankly, I don't want one either."

"What? Why?" She glanced at her friend, confused by Ginger's confession.

"Look, it's not in the grand plan for me. I'm happy for my brother. After everything we've been through, he deserves the happiness his mates are bringing him." Ginger made her way down the hall then stepped into the back room.

Brienne scrunched up her nose. "Why are you lying?"

Ginger slammed the cupboard door. "I'm not lying. I really do want to be left alone."

"No you don't," Brie whispered. "You're saying it so you believe it. But, you don't mean it."

"Shut up, Brie." Ginger wiped her eyes. "You have no idea what I want. No one does. So, how about you keep your opinions to yourself."

"What happened to you?" Brie came up behind her friend and laid her hand on Ginger's shoulder.

"Nothing happened to me." She poured the hot

water into two cups. "What makes you think anything happened to me?"

"I don't," Brie stated sarcastically. "Maybe because of how defensive you got. The fact you're crying and trying to hide it. What happened?"

"Why do you care? You're leaving, aren't you?" her friend questioned. "It's the latest rumor flying around."

She supposed Ginger was right. "I'm not sure what I'm going to do. A part of me wants to stay while the other part of me is still afraid of what will happen if I do."

Ginger snorted. "You left before the worst of everything started with Magnum. You have nothing to fear anymore."

"And you?"

"I have everything to be afraid of."

"Then it looks like I have my work cut out for me. You have nothing to be scared of anymore, Ginger Silver, and I'm going to prove it." Determination filled Brie as she sat at the small table watching her friend move around the space. "Now, why don't you start from the beginning and tell me why you feel unworthy of love."

Determination filled her when she walked out of the bookstore. The idea of leaving her life behind in Rosewood scared the shit out of her, but the conversation with Ginger still fresh in her mind cemented the need to stay with her pack. Because, her friend was right, she didn't have anything to worry about. She hadn't been abused or raped or whatever happened to the others. She hadn't woken up day after day wondering if today would be the day she'd be harmed or tortured.

No, Lance wouldn't allow anyone in his pack to suffer. A part of her called herself selfish for having such an amazing place to hide. Getting into the truck, she used the vehicle's GPS and plotted her way to Black Hills College. If she left now, she could return in time to meet Shawn for their date.

Brienne grinned.

All the anxiety about coming home and spending time with her family washed away. When she finished her errands, she'd call Lance and have her things sent to Rapid City. She didn't have to leave.

The drive would only take an hour or so. Already she began to make lists of things she needed to do and things she'd need for her practice. As it stood, she could get her therapy license, not like she needed it for the pack, but it would be nice to hang in her office and say she'd done it on her own. She also needed an office. *Tomorrow you can figure it out.* A smile tugged at her lips. *Honey, I'm home.*

Chapter Ten

They raced through the forest. A lightness Shawn hadn't seen in his mate lit his soul. When Brie had picked him up a few hours ago from Gee's, his blood sang through his veins. She teased him in the bar then placed a searing kiss upon his lips, tempting him even more. Curiosity filled him. He had questions for her, but every time he tried to voice them, he took one look at his mate, and they disappeared.

Later, he'd ask her. After he got her to the clearing. After they made love.

Shawn nipped at her hind legs before bounding over the downed log to take the lead, Brienne, right behind him, nudging him every so often. As they came to the clearing, he stopped. His mate bounced into him and, as he shifted to his human form, he laughed. Gathered in his arms to protect her, she shifted as well. She giggled, holding onto him while they came to a rolling stop.

"What has gotten into you." Shawn brushed a lock of her hair out of her face. "You're feisty tonight."

Brie shrugged. "It was a good day."

"Oh?" He kissed her. He brushed his fingers down the column of her spine then teased the cleft of her ass.

"Yes." Her eyes fluttered shut, and she arched to him. "I made a few decisions today."

"Really? Are you going to tell me, mate?"

"I suppose. Would you like to hear them now or later?" She fit her hand between them and fisted his cock.

"Later." He groaned. "Definitely later." She stroked the length of his erection as he kissed a path across her jaw and down her neck.

"I thought you might want to wait."

He kissed her again with a ferocious hunger he'd never experienced before. He didn't sip from her lips, he feasted on her. Devoured her with each pump of his tongue. She whimpered then whispered his name, writhing against him. "Mine," he growled.

"Yours," she laughed.

He rolled them, so she lay under him and pinned her to the ground. "You are up to something." He nuzzled her neck. "I can smell it," he murmured before drawing the lobe of her ear into his mouth.

"I'm not. I promise."

"Mmhmm." He slid down her body and covered her nipple with his mouth. He rasped his tongue over the tight bead and reveled in the soft mewling sound she made in her throat. "I believe you're lying to me now." He moved over to the other nipple and applied the same attention.

Her fingers raked through his hair. She panted softly, shaking her head. "Nope. I'll tell you later."

"Where is the fun in that?" He shifted his weight then skimmed his hand over her hip. Cupping her sex, he slid his finger through her folds and was rewarded by her wetness.

"I have other fun things I'd rather do right now," she whined. "Later, I promised."

"I say you should tell me." He buried a second finger inside her and wiggled the digits.

"Oh my." She arched to him.

"Indeed." He took her nipple into his mouth, then bit the peak. "Tell me. I love seeing you this excited, mate."

"After." She moaned his name and arched to him. "Make love to me. Please, Shawn."

"I like it when you say please." He rubbed at her sweet spot. Her hips bucked, and a cry of pleasure fell from her lips.

"I'm saying please," she whimpered. "Do it."

He chuckled. Even though his dick ached and balls were drawn up close to his body, he enjoyed turning her on. Making her squirm and blissed out of her mind. He kissed her side. "I will. When I'm ready."

Shawn opened her to his perusal then placed her legs over his shoulders. He took a deep breath and let out a ragged groan. Her spicy scent went straight to his groin, thickening his cock. *Give me strength.* He nuzzled her sex before running his tongue through her slit and gathering up her cream.

"Shawn," she sobbed.

"I've got you, little Brie," he muttered. Her swollen clit pulsed with need. Drawing the hard nub into his mouth he lashed the bundle of nerves.

Brienne screamed. She squeezed her legs,

trapping him between them.

"I love how responsive you are to my touch." He licked her again before settling in.

Fire raced through his veins. The way her body reacted to his touch went to his head, leaving him dizzy with need. He placed a kiss to her clit then climbed up her body. He couldn't take the pressure building inside him any longer. "Hold on, Brie." Shawn positioned himself at her entrance and pushed forward.

The searing heat of her pussy along with her wetness threatened to destroy his control. He retreated and filled her again. Each thrust taking him deeper, her tight pussy fisting his dick. Brienne thrashed below him, her pleas were incoherent as he stilled and cupped her cheek. Her blue eyes sparkled with arousal and desire. He didn't want to move. He wanted to etch this moment into his brain for all time.

"I'm staying." Her bottom lip trembled. "I don't want to leave."

Her admission caught him off guard but spurred the lust coursing through him. "Fuck, what a thing to say, right now," he chuckled. He shifted his hips. "I'm happy, babe. So fucking happy." He lowered his face to her neck and buried it there as he picked up his pace. The intensity of his emotions surprised the fuck out of him.

"I love you, Brie." He thrust into her, needing to mate her and mark her for everyone to see.

"I love you, too, Shawn," she cried out, scoring her fingers across his shoulders, holding onto him for dear life.

Shawn lifted her leg over his hip and he slid even

farther into her. He saw stars. His breath left him on a whoosh as she clenched around him. She rippled around him, signaling her impending climax, and he grew more excited. "Let go, Brienne. I've got you."

Her body tightened around his, holding him close. She sucked in a breath, and as he reached between them to play with her clit, she shouted. Her pussy convulsed and pulsed around him while her body jerked. Her soft cries undid him. He filled her two more times before biting her mark.

She climaxed again, this time harder. Her muscles tugged at his cock, milking him. He gave over to the sensation. He groaned while licking the mark on her neck, enjoying the way she went pliant below him.

Holding her close, he closed his eyes and breathed in his mate's scent. He was a lucky son of a bitch. Nothing would separate them again and no one would ever come between them no matter what.

Sometime later after returning to Shawn's home, well, hers, too, now, Brie stared at her mate. The night before had been amazing. Exquisite. She never got around to explaining to her mate what she'd planned for herself. But she figured when he finally woke up, she'd be able to.

"Hey." He opened his eyes, and stretched before pulling her closer to his chest. His masculine scent wrapped around her in a blanket of protection.

"Good morning."

"Did you sleep well?" He palmed her hip and squeezed.

"I did, better than I have in a long time." She

shifted them so she could lay her head on his chest. The steady beat of his heart comforted her. "I have a plan."

"So you were saying last night."

"I'm going to school at Black Hills College. I start next week."

"Good. As much as I would follow you anywhere, mate, I didn't want to leave our pack." At least he'd been honest with her. Even though he'd been telling the truth when he told her he'd leave Los Lobos, it would cause him distress.

"I realized yesterday while talking to Ginger, I couldn't leave. The things that happened here...." She sighed and shook her head. "So much pain lingers within our pack. If I can help one person or three people, it'll be worth it."

"The pack will be grateful you're here." He kissed the crown of her head and hugged her. "I have a job now, too. Or I should say I officially have a job."

"Oh?" She propped herself up on her elbow. "Do tell."

"I'm going to be working with Saja. She wants to bring more people home. I have the resources to help do so. It's a win-win for the pack." He trailed his fingers up and down her back. "It's who I was talking to yesterday."

"Excellent!" she exclaimed. "I am sure there are several families here who can benefit from your help as well."

"I hope so." He rolled her under him. "But, right now, I have something else I want to talk to you about."

Shawn settled between her legs and probed her entrance with the tip of his cock. "What?"

"Marry me. Make an honest wolf out of me."

Excitement filled Brie. Her heart skipped a beat. "Really?"

"Yes, really," he laughed. "Marry me."

She squealed as happiness warmed her from the inside out. "Yes. I'll marry you."

"Hot damn." His hips shifted and he filled her in one thrust. "I've waited almost my whole life for you. I ain't ever letting you go. I love you, little Brie."

"I'm not letting you go either, Shawn. I love you, too."

Epilogue

Three weeks later

Fern waved as Kathy, Claire, and Lonnie made their way through the maze of tables. Another couple was happily mated, thanks to her and the ladies. A job well done if she did say so herself. Plus, Claire had her niece home. If only Claire's daughter and son were there, they'd be all set, but, one step at a time. One day at a time.

As the women sat down, Paul came over to the table and greeted them. "Good afternoon, my boy." Fern smiled. "A round of beers for us. We're celebrating." The waiter cocked a brow. "Don't worry. Henry's picking us up if we got too unruly." She winked at him, and he shook his head.

"I am so happy for Brienne and Shawn. Now Claire can plan a wedding."

"I'm sitting this one out." Claire played with her amber necklace. "Brienne wants me to relax and bask in the happiness. I intend to."

Lonnie laughed. "I bet. After the fracas they

made in the woods the other night. I wouldn't be surprised if she didn't get knocked up sooner rather than later."

"Ah, young love." Kathy sighed.

"It is beautiful," Fern agreed.

"So, she's staying, then," Lonnie questioned. "I know Brienne and Shawn are mated, but the last I heard, she wanted to finish school."

"She's staying." Claire smiled. "She'll be finishing at Black Hills College. Lance sent her stuff to the post office in Rapid City so she didn't have to return."

"Wonderful." Fern clapped her hands. "So, who is our next couple?"

"Ginger," Kathy said. "I heard she's been talking to Brienne."

"Oh?" Lonnie arched a brow. "How is it going?"

"Good." Paul brought their drinks and placed them on the table. "Thank you, Paul." The mute waiter nodded and headed off to another table. "From what I've heard, Ginger is making progress. Not sure how much though."

"I heard Jasper is having a hard time now." Claire frowned. "Kole and Max were going to talk to Drew about allowing a family visit."

"Really?" Fern questioned. "Who?"

"His brother. I think Kole said his name is Mark."

"Hmm...." Fern tapped her chin. "If he looks anything like Jasper, I'm sure Ginger might be interested. Wouldn't you agree?"

"What would Ginger be interested in?" Gee's deep voice surprised Fern. "What are you ladies up to? You never drink this early."

"We're celebrating. We're allowed." Claire gave

him a haughty glance.

"We're also helping a friend out," Lonnie added. "In fact, I bet we could help you out, too."

Fear clouded Gee's eyes. "Nope, not happening."

"Oh come on, Gee. It'll be fun." Kathy winked at him. "You need to unclench like half the wolves around here."

"There is a tenderhearted omega who could use a little TLC only a bear like yourself could administer." Lonnie gave him a saucy wink. "What do you say?"

Gee pulled a face. "Horse shit," he snarled. "Leave me out of your games." He stomped away from their table before the women erupted in laughter.

"Well done, ladies," Fern cheered while the others continued to laugh. "Well done."

"So, do we have our next match, then?" Kathy steered them back to the topic they'd abandoned when Gee interrupted them.

"I think so." Claire nodded.

"I agree." Lonnie tipped her bee toward Kathy.

"Then it's a match," Fern supplied.

Movement out of the corner of her eye made her look up. Shawn, with Brie in tow, stopped beside them. Both looked well mated and happy together. She grinned at them then offered the remaining chairs. "What can we do for you?"

"Brienne has some information for you." Shawn took a seat after helping his mate into her chair.

"I wanted to tell you sooner." Brienne's cheeks turned a cute shade of pink. "But, I didn't...well I wasn't sure how to tell you, with everything going on. I kind of put it on the back burner."

"We understand." Claire took her niece's hand.

"What is it?"

Brienne took a deep breath then let it out slow. "I know where your son and daughter are," she stated. "I got an email from Jason yesterday."

Claire's eyes went wide. Her skin paled. If she hadn't been situated between Lonnie and Kathy, Fern worried she'd fall over. "Jason?" Claire whispered. "Is...is he okay?"

"He's fine. He's in Maine. Portland, to be exact. Sarah is with him and, well, they want to come home. They miss you."

"Wonderful news." Fern smacked the table. "Gee, we're going to need another round of drinks here!"

Brienne wrapped her arms around Claire. They held each other tight. "I can't believe it. When will they be here?"

"Couple of days. Drew's been made aware they're coming home. Ryker's meeting them at the border of the pack lands." Brienne held tight to her aunt.

"Well, I'll be," Claire murmured. "I guess I'd better tell Joe."

"Tell me what?" Joe loomed over his mate. His whiskey eyes filled with curiosity. "If you're wondering, Gee called. Told me you were drunk."

"Pish." Lonnie snorted. "We've only begun. The old fuddy-duddy."

"Brienne and Shawn found Jason and Sarah," Claire blurted. "They're coming home."

"Hot damn!" Joe hollered then tugged his mate into his arms and spun her around in a circle. "I can't wait." He kissed Claire soundly and the bar erupted in catcalls and wolf whistles.

"Get a room, you two," Gee yelled from the bar. "And not the side of my bar either!"

Fern laughed along with everyone at the table. "At this rate, we'll be partying all night."

"Next round's on me," Shawn lifted his hand to signal Paul.

"Why, Mr. Blu, are you planning on getting us drunk today?" Kathy questioned, with a coy grin.

Shawn laughed. "Ma'am, your mate would tan my hide. Now, Brienne, on the other hand, well...."

The girl giggled and swatted at her mate. "You're trying to get lucky, aren't you, mate?"

"Indeed I am, Miss Talbert. Indeed I am."

About the Author

TL Reeve, a multi-published author with Cobblestone Press, Decadent Publishing, Evernight Publishing, and Loose-Id, was born out of a love of family and a bond that became unbreakable. Living in Alabama, TL misses Los Angeles, and will one day return to the beaches of Southern California to ride the waves at Huntington Beach. When not writing something hot and sexy, TL can be found curled up with a good book, or working on homework with a cute little pixie.

You can signup for her newsletter at: http://eepurl.com/bvo7fn

Also by TL Reeve